Mary Shelley

FRANKENSTEIN

Text adaptation by Maud Jackson
Task-based analysis by Guglielmo Corrado

D1726121

Editors: Elvira Poggi, Rebecca Raynes
Design: Nadia Maestri
Illustrations: Gianni De Conno

© Cideb Editrice S.r.l.
Rapallo - Italy 1997

ISBN 3-425-03095-7

© 1998 Verlag Moritz Diesterweg GmbH & Co., Frankfurt am Main.
Alle Rechte vorbehalten. Das Werk und seine Teile sind urheberrechtlich geschützt. Jede
Verwertung in anderen als den gesetzlich zugelassenen Fällen bedarf deshalb der
vorherigen schriftlichen Einwilligung des Verlags.

Druck und Verarbeitung: Zechnersche Buchdruckerei, Speyer
Printed in Germany

Contents

This story is recorded in full on cassettes.

Chronology

1797   Mary Wollstonecraft Godwin is born on 30 August, the daughter of Mary Wollstonecraft, a famous feminist, and of the philosopher William Godwin.
Twelve days after her birth, her mother dies of puerperal fever.

1801   William Godwin marries Mary Jane Clairmont, a widow with two children.

1812   Percy Bysshe Shelley arranges a meeting with William Godwin and sees Mary for the first time. Shelley's marriage with Harriet Westbrook is failing.

1814   Shelley and Mary flee to France, arousing public indignation.

1815   On 22 February, Mary gives birth prematurely to a baby girl, Clara, who dies after a few weeks.

Chronology

1816 On 24 January Mary gives birth to a son, William.

Claire Clairmont, Mary's step-sister, becomes Lord Byron's lover. Shelley, Mary and Clare Clairmont move to Switzerland and settle at Champagne Chapuis, near Byron's villa.

On 16 June, the 'waking dream', which gives rise to *Frankenstein*, takes place.

On 30 December, after Harriet's suicide, Mary and Percy get married.

1817 On 14 May Mary completes *Frankenstein*.

She gives birth to a daughter, Clara Everina.

1818 Publication of *Frankenstein*.

The Shelleys settle in Italy. Their daughter Clara Everina dies in Venice.

1819 Their son William dies of malaria.

The Shelleys spend a period in Rome and in Florence.

Mary gives birth to Percy Florence.

1820 They move to Pisa.

Mary begins her novel *Valperga*.

1822 The Shelleys settle at Casa Magni near Lerici.

P.B. Shelley dies during a storm, while sailing with a friend and his body is burnt on the beach.

1823 Mary returns to England.
Publication of her novel *Valperga*.

1826 Publication of her novel *The Last Man*.

1830 Publication of her novel *Perkin Warbeck*.

1831 Publication of the revised edition of *Frankenstein*.

1851 On 1 February Mary dies in London and is buried in St. Peter's churchyard, Bournemouth.

FRANKENSTEIN;

or,

THE MODERN PROMETHEUS.

IN THREE VOLUMES.

Did I request thee, Maker, from my clay
To mould me man? Did I solicit thee
From darkness to promote me?——
PARADISE LOST.

VOL. I.

London:
PRINTED FOR
LACKINGTON, HUGHES, HARDING, MAVOR, & JONES,
FINSBURY SQUARE.

1818.

Genesis of Frankenstein

In her introduction to the 1831 edition of *Frankenstein*, Mary W. Shelley gave her own account of its origins. Firstly, she underlined her tendency to 'the formation of castles in the air – the indulging in waking dreams – the following trains of thoughts, which had for their subject the formation of a succession of imaginary incidents'. [1] Then, she gave relevance to the fact that she was born into a family of distinguished literary celebrity and Shelley wanted her to write her own 'page of fame'. [1]

It is certain that in the summer of 1816, Percy Shelley, Mary Godwin and Claire Clairmont left for Geneva and settled at Champagne Chapuis, a cottage on the shores of the lake which was not far from Villa Diodati, where the English poet Lord Byron was living.

In June, as the weather was very rainy and wet, the Shelleys and Byron spent much time together. Inside Byron's villa they started reading some French translations of German ghost stories. It happened that one of those nights Byron proposed that each of them should write a ghost story and so Mary busied herself 'to think of a story... one which would speak to the mysterious fears of nature, and awaken thrilling horror'. [1]

In fact, a sort of 'waking dream' is said to have given Mary the idea of *Frankenstein*, which she developed into a novel, urged on by Shelley.

In September, they returned to England and Mary went on working on the novel until May, 1817.

The first edition of *Frankenstein* appeared on 11th March, 1818.

---

1. *Letter* by Mary Wollstonecraft Shelley dated October 15, 1831.

Filmography

Frankenstein by James S. Dowley, starring Charles Ogle (USA, 1910).

Frankenstein by James Whale, starring Boris Karloff (The Creature), Colin Clive (Frankenstein), Dwight Frye, Edward Van Sloan, (USA, 1931).

The Bride of Frankenstein by James Whale, starring Boris Karloff, Colin Clive, Valerie Hobson, Elsa Lanchester, John Carradine (USA, 1935).

Son of Frankenstein by Rowland V. Lee, starring Boris Karloff, Bela Lugosi, Basil Rathbone (USA, 1939).

Ghost of Frankenstein by Erle C. Kenton, starring Bela Lugosi, Lon Chaney jr., Cedric Hardwicke, Evelyn Ankers (USA, 1942).

Frankenstein Meets the Wolf Man by Roy W. Neill, starring Bela Lugosi, Lon Chaney jr., Maria Ouspenskaja, Lionel Atwill, Ilona Massey (USA, 1943).

House of Frankenstein by Erle C. Kenton, starring John Carradine, Glenn Strange, Lon Chaney jr., Boris Karloff, Lionel Atwill (USA, 1944).

Curse of Frankenstein by Terence Fisher, starring Peter Cushing, Christopher Lee (Great Britain, 1956).

The Revenge of Frankenstein by Terence Fisher, starring Peter Cushing, Jack Watson (Great Britain, 1957).

Frankenstein '70 by Howard W. Koch, starring Boris Karloff, Tom Duggan, Jana Lund (USA, 1958).

Evil of Frankenstein by Freddie Francis, starring Peter Cushing, Kiwi Kingston (Great Britain, 1963).

Frankenstein Created Woman by Terence Fisher, starring Peter Cushing, Thorley Walters, Susan Denberg (Great Britain, 1966).

Filmography

Frankenstein Must Be Destroyed by Terence Fisher, starring Peter Cushing, Freddie Jones (Great Britain, 1969).

The Horror of Frankenstein by Al Adamson, starring J. Carrol Naish, Lon Chaney jr., Forrest J. Ackermann (Great Britain, 1970).

The Bride by Frank Roddam, starring Sting, Jennifer Beals (USA, 1985).

Gothic by Ken Russel, starring Gabriel Byrne, Julian Sands, Natasha Richardson (Great Britain, 1986).

Frankenstein Unbound by Roger Corman, starring John Hurt, Raul Julia, Bridget Fonda (USA, 1990).

Frankenstein: the Real Story by David Wickes, starring Patrick Bergin, Randy Quaid (Great Britain, 1992).

Frankenstein by Kenneth Branagh, starring Robert De Niro, Helena Bonham Carter (USA,1994).

Before reading

1 What do you already know about Frankenstein?
Have you ever seen any films about him?
Tell your classmates what you already know.

2 What are your ambitions about the future?
Put the following ambitions in order of importance, then compare
your list with your classmates.

☐ to study hard so as to become a famous person
☐ to get married and have children
☐ to be rich
☐ to be popular
☐ to find a good job
☐ to travel a lot
☐ to have an adventurous life

Do you think that being very ambitious might cause problems?
Discuss your answers with your classmates.

3 Read the following definition of the word *letter*:

letter: a written message addressed to a person or an organization,
usually put in an envelope and sent by post.

A letter may be written in different registers. What are they?

4 Look at the following pictures and try to define the 3 elements involved in this form of communication.

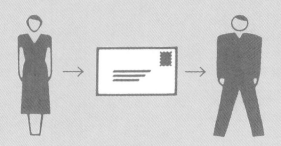

Addresser =

Letter =

Addressee =

Check your answers in your monolingual dictionary.

Letter One

To Mrs Margaret Saville, England
                St Petersburgh, 11 December 17—
My dear sister,
    I arrived here yesterday, in good health and full
of hope. The cold wind from the north fills me   5
with excitement. I dream of the North Pole, the
goal of my voyage. In my dream it is a beautiful
place where the sun never sets, and I will be the
first man to walk upon its virgin snow. I am not

10 *afraid of danger or death. Who knows? I might find a passage to the East that will help our traders, or perhaps I will discover something useful to science. So do not worry about me, Margaret. You know that I always wanted to be*
15 *an explorer, except for the few years when I tried to be a poet and failed. Ever since I inherited my fortune six years ago, I have dreamt of this voyage. In two weeks I will go to Archangel to hire a ship and a crew. In June we will sail*
20 *north. When will I return to you? I do not know. If I succeed, years will pass before we meet again. If I fail, you will see me soon or never.*

Goodbye, my dear Margaret.

Your affectionate brother,
R. Walton
25

1 **In the letter you have just read who is:**

- the addresser?
- the addressee?

2 **Underline the correct information below about the addresser:**

Physical conditions	in bad/good/fairly good health
Character	shy/adventurous/afraid/brave/ ambitious/enthusiastic/unbearable
Monetary situation	poor/rich/millionaire/desperate/ beggar
Place where the letter was written	England/St Petersburgh/ North Pole/Archangel
Next destination of the person writing	England/St Petersburgh/ North Pole/Archangel
Reason for the voyage	to visit his sister/to hire a ship/ to settle there
Time of departure from Archangel	on 11th December/in June/ the following day
Previous occupation	teacher/poet/mariner/writer/captain
Present occupation	teacher/poet/mariner/writer/captain
Relationship between addresser and addressee	father and mother/brother and sister/friends/husband and wife

Before reading

1 While listening to letters 2 and 3, put a cross in the correct column:

	True	False
a. Walton has hired a ship	☐	☐
b. Walton has lots of friends	☐	☐
c. Walton hopes to meet friends in Archangel	☐	☐
d. Walton is excited	☐	☐
e. Walton doesn't like receiving letters	☐	☐
f. It is autumn	☐	☐
g. Warm winds blow from the North	☐	☐
h. Walton is hopeful	☐	☐

Check your answers by reading the text and correct the false sentences.

2 What do you associate with the word *devil*?
Complete the following spidergram then compare it with your classmates'.

Walton's Letters

Letter Two

To Mrs Saville, England

Archangel, 28 March 17—

I have hired a ship and crew. The men are brave and diligent, but I have no friend. I have no one to talk to about my hopes and fears. I will not find a friend here at Archangel or on the sea.

As I wait for the voyage to begin, I am full of excitement. Sometimes I am happy. At other times I am afraid. Will I see you again, dear Margaret? Write to me often. Your letters comfort me. If you never hear from me again, remember me with affection.

Your brother,
Robert Walton

Walton's Letters

Letter Three

To Mrs Saville, England

7 July 17—

My dear sister,
The voyage has begun at last. I am well and in
good spirits [1]. Although great sheets of ice float
past us on the sea, it is summer, and warm winds
blow us north. Now I feel sure that I will succeed!
Goodbye, Margaret!

R.W.

1. **in good spirits** : happy.

Letter Four

To Mrs Saville, England

5 August 17—

I must tell you about the strange thing that has
happened. Last Monday we were surrounded by ice.
The ship could not move. We were very far from land.   5
We waited anxiously, looking out at the ice, which
stretched to the horizon. Suddenly, we saw a sledge[1]
pulled by dogs going north. A gigantic man drove the
sledge. We watched until he disappeared from sight.

Later the ice broke, and we were able to move   10
again. The next morning, we found another sledge
on a floating sheet of ice in the sea. The man in
this sledge was weak, tired, and half-frozen. We

1. **sledge** : vehicle used for travelling over snow.

invited him onto the ship, but he said, 'Tell me
15 *first where you are going.' When I told him we*
were going north, he climbed onto the ship. We
gave him food and warm clothes. For two days he
was very ill, and I feared he had gone mad. When
he had recovered a little, I asked him what he was
20 *doing alone on the ice.*

'I am following someone,' he said.

'Someone who is also travelling alone on a
sledge?' I asked.

'Yes.'

25 *'Then I think we have seen him.'*

He asked many questions about 'the devil', as he
called the other man. Which way was he
travelling? Did I think that the breaking of the ice
had destroyed the other sledge? From that moment,
30 *he was full of energy and purpose. He is an*
interesting man, and I like him very much. I wrote
in one of my letters that I would not find a friend
on the sea, but maybe I was wrong. I cannot send
this letter, so I will continue it as a journal¹ to
35 *send you when I can.*

---

1. **journal** : diary.

Journal Sections

13 August 17—

*The man's name is Victor Frankenstein. I like him more
every day. I admire him and pity him. He speaks well, he is
intelligent and sensitive, but he has some secret sadness.*

    Now that he is a little stronger, he spends all his time on   5
*the deck, watching for the other sledge. I watch with him,
talking about my hopes for this voyage. One day I told him of
my ambitions to gain knowledge and succeed where other men
have failed. My words disturbed him.*

    'Unhappy man!' he said, 'Do you share my madness? Let   10
me tell you my story, and I hope it will be a warning to you.'

    He was too ill to continue.

Journal Sections

19 August 17—

    Yesterday the stranger said to me, 'I have had a very unhappy life. I want to tell my story to you, because you too are ambitious. You want knowledge and wisdom, as I once did.' Today he will begin to tell me his tale. Every night I will write down his words. You must be eager [1] *to read his story. Think, then, how eager I am. I know him. I can hear his wonderful voice and see his shining eyes. How awful must be the tale that has ruined such a man!*

---

1. **eager** : enthusiastic, interested.

1 After reading Letter 4 complete the following sentences.

a. On Monday the ship could not move because ....

b. The crew saw a sledge which was driven by ....

c. The ship was able to move again because ....

d. The next morning the crew found ....

e. The driver of the sledge was ....

f. The man got on board after asking ....

g. The man was ill for ....

h. Some time later the man explained that he was following ....

i. The man asked for information about ....

j. Walton liked the man and thought he had found ....

Journal Sections

2 Look back at the 2 journal sections and complete this chart.

Man's name	
Man's characteristics	
Man's reaction to Walton's ambition	
Why the man started telling his story	
Man's previous life	
What sort of story Walton expects to hear	

Chapter One

Frankenstein's Narrative

I was born in Geneva. My father was a magistrate.[1] I had a little brother called William and an adopted sister called Elizabeth. My parents found Elizabeth living with a poor family in Italy. She was gentle and very beautiful, with golden hair and blue eyes. Her real parents, an Italian nobleman and a German lady, were both dead. My mother and father adopted Elizabeth and brought her to our home.

Elizabeth and I grew up together, and we were very happy. I spent my days with Elizabeth, William, and my dear friend

---

1. **magistrate** : an official who acts as a judge in the lowest courts.

Chapter One

Henry Clerval. Henry wanted to be a poet. He loved nature and beauty, but I was interested in science. I wished to make some great scientific discovery. I wanted wisdom and knowledge, and I wanted to succeed where other men had failed.

When I was seventeen, my parents decided to send me to the university at Ingolstadt, but my departure was delayed by the first misfortune of my life. Elizabeth became ill with scarlet fever, [1] and my mother nursed her. Slowly Elizabeth recovered, but my mother caught the illness from her. When my poor mother was dying, she called us to her bedside and said, 'Dear Victor and Elizabeth, your father and I hope that one day you two will marry. Be happy, my children, and take care of little William.'

She died calmly. How can I describe our sadness? There is no need. Everyone knows that sadness, or will know it one day. A few weeks later I went to the university in Ingolstadt. I walked around the town during the first three days. I met some of my professors and fellow students, but I felt lonely and disappointed. I had no desire to study. Then I went to hear a lecture by Mr Waldman, the professor of chemistry. At the end of the lecture, he spoke of modern chemistry in words I will never forget.

'Modern chemists can perform miracles,' he said. 'They have followed Nature to her hiding places. They have

---

1. **scarlet fever** : a very serious, infectious disease.

35 penetrated her secrets. They have discovered how the blood
circulates. They understand the nature of thunder storms and
earthquakes. They are like gods.'

Those were the professor's words — or the words of Fate [1]
— spoken to destroy me. I left the lecture full of a new
40 ambition. 'I will discover new things in science,' I thought.
'I will explain the mysteries of creation.'

The next day I went to Mr Waldman. 'I wish to be your
student,' I said. He showed me his laboratory and told me
what books to read. My future was decided.

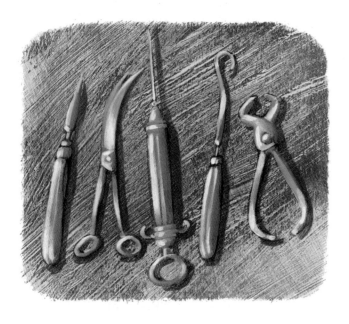

1. **Fate** : destiny.

1 Look back at Chapter 1 and do the following activity. Captain Walton has asked Victor Frankenstein some questions. The following are Frankenstein's answers. Write Walton's questions.

Walton: ....?
Frankenstein: I was born in Geneva.
Walton: ....?
Frankenstein: I had a little brother called William and an adopted sister called Elizabeth.
Walton: ....?
Frankenstein: An Italian nobleman and a German lady.
Walton: ....?
Frankenstein: No, I also spent my days with my friend Clerval.
Walton: ....?
Frankenstein: Henry was interested in nature and beauty.
Walton: ....?
Frankenstein: When I was 17, but my departure was delayed.
Walton: ....?
Frankenstein: Because my mother caught scarlet fever from Elizabeth and died.
Walton: ....?
Frankenstein: She expressed the wish that we would be married.
Walton: ....?
Frankenstein: I went to Ingolstadt.
Walton: ....?
Frankenstein: No, I did not like studying.
Walton: ....?
Frankenstein: When I listened to a lecture by professor Waldman.
Walton: ....?
Frankenstein: He talked about modern chemistry.
Walton: ....?
Frankenstein: I felt fascinated.
Walton: ....?
Frankenstein: I decided to discover new things in science.

Chapter Two

I was a diligent [1] student. I became very interested in the human body. 'Where does life come from?' I asked myself. To study life you must also study death. I began to work with dead bodies. I studied the progress of their decay. [2] I examined the change from life to death and from death to life. Then one day I suddenly understood. I was surprised that nobody had discovered the secret before. I had succeeded where other men had failed.

I am not mad. I swear it is true. After days and nights of work, I discovered how life was created. I, myself was able to create life.

1. **diligent** : hard-working.
2. **decay** : decomposition, deterioration.

Chapter Two

I can see by your eager expression, my friend, that you
want me to tell you the secret. I will not tell you, and soon
you will understand why not. Listen to my story, and learn
from my example. Knowledge is dangerous. An ambitious man
is not a happy man.

My first task was to create a body. I worked day and night. I
grew thin and pale, but I continued to work. The moon watched
me through the window as I uncovered the secrets of Nature.
What horrible work it was! I explored dead bodies and tortured
living animals, but my work did not seem horrible to me then. I
thought that I had conquered death. I would be the creator of a
new race of happy and excellent creatures!

All summer I worked on my filthy [1] creation in a lonely
attic room. I did not see the sunshine, the flowers, or the
green leaves. I did not write to my family or think about them.
I thought only of my work.

Any ambition that makes you forget the people you love
and the simple pleasures of ordinary life is bad. The leaves
fell from the trees, and still I worked. I became anxious and
nervous. I avoided other people. I hid myself like a criminal.
My creation was nearly done. Soon it would be finished, and
then, I promised myself, I would rest and recover my health.

1.   **filthy** : (here) corrupt, vile.

1 **Read carefully, then fill in the gaps in the following summary using the adjectives in the bell jar below:**

Victor was a .... student, interested in the
.... body.

He started to work with .... bodies.

One day he discovered how to create life.

While telling Walton his story Victor remarks that knowledge is
.... and that an .... man is ....

Victor worked day and night and became .... and pale.
He explored .... bodies and tortured ....
animals. He was convinced that he would create a new race of happy
and .... creatures.

He worked in a .... attic all summer without even
writing to his family.

Little by little he became .... and nervous and avoided
meeting people.

His creation was almost complete.

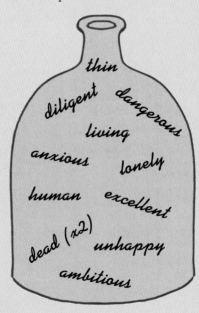

thin
diligent dangerous
living
anxious lonely
human excellent
dead (x2) unhappy
ambitious

2 **Write all the names of monsters you know, thinking of:**

- other times (for example the Prehistoric age)
- other planets (for example Mars)
- other countries (for example Scotland)
- novels, television and films

Compare your list of names with your classmates. Whose list is the most original?

Before reading

1 Look at the picture below and describe the monster in your exercise book.

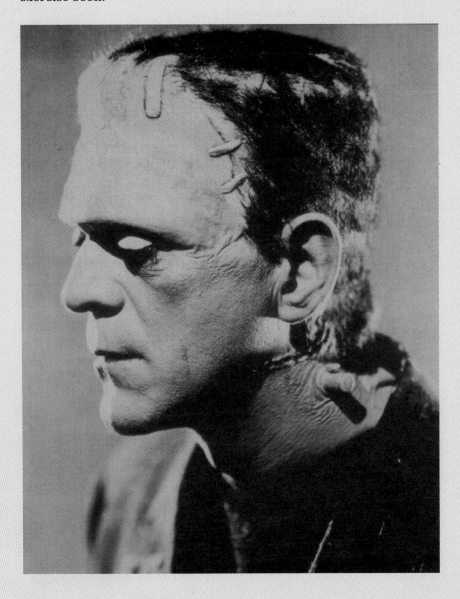

2 Listen carefully to the first section of Chapter 3 (lines 1-19) and complete the following grid:

Weather	
Time of day	
Month	
Time when the creature awoke	
What the creature's skin was like	
What the creature's hair was like	
What the creature's eyes were like	
How long Victor had worked	
Victor's feelings at seeing the creature	
Victor's reaction at seeing the creature	

Check your answers by reading the text.

3 Tick as appropriate, then compare your choices with your neighbour's.
What sort of atmosphere is created?

☐ happy
☐ dark and gloomy
☐ quiet
☐ dramatic
☐ tragic

4 What devices does the writer use to create this particular atmosphere?

☐ positive connotations
☐ particular nouns
☐ use of colours
☐ negative connotations

Chapter Three

I completed my creation one cold rainy night in November. With trembling hands I gathered my instruments to give life to the dead thing that lay at my feet. It was one o'clock in the morning when, by the light of the candle, I saw the yellow eye of the creature open. He breathed. He moved.

How can I describe him? I had tried to make him beautiful. Great God! His skin was yellow and

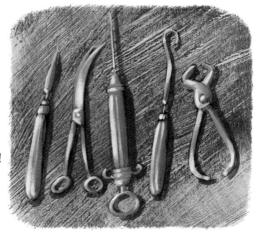

5

Frankenstein's Narrative

wrinkled. His hair was long and black. His eyes were watery.
15 He was monstrous!

I had worked for nearly two years for this moment. Now
that the moment had come, I felt nothing but horror and
disgust. I ran out of the room. For hours I lay awake in my
bedroom, horrified by what I had done.

20 When at last I fell asleep, I dreamt that I saw Elizabeth,
young and healthy, walking in the streets of Ingolstadt.
Delighted and surprised, I embraced her, but when I kissed
her she grew pale and cold. Her face began to change into the
face of my dead mother. She was wrapped in a shroud, 1 and
25 I saw the grave-worms crawling in its folds.

I woke up trembling with horror. My forehead was cold
with sweat. By the pale yellow light of the moon, I saw the
monster I had created. He was standing beside my bed,
looking down at me. He made a sound, grinned at me, and
30 stretched out his hand to touch me. I ran away and spent the
rest of the night outside.

The next morning was grey and rainy. I walked the streets
of Ingolstadt, afraid to return to my apartment. Suddenly I
heard someone call my name. Turning round, I saw Henry

---

1. **shroud** : a sheet to cover a dead body.

Frankenstein's Narrative

35 Clerval stepping out of the coach [1] that had just arrived from Geneva.

'My dear Frankenstein!' he cried. 'I am so glad to see you! I have come to study at the university.'

We walked to my apartment together. I asked him about my
40 father, Elizabeth, and William.

'They are all well, but they are a little worried because you do not write to them,' he said. Then he stopped and looked at me anxiously. 'But my dear Frankenstein, you are ill! You are so pale and thin!'

45 I told him that I had been working too much. I did not want to think about what had happened the night before. I was afraid to see the monster again, but I was even more afraid

---

1. **coach** : horse-drawn carriage for transporting paying passengers from one town to another.

Chapter Three

that Henry would see him. When we came to my apartment,
I left Henry at the door. I ran upstairs and into my room,
trembling with fear. The apartment was empty. Relieved,   50
I called Henry and told him to come upstairs.

'Victor, what is the matter?' asked Henry.

I covered my face with my hands and said, 'Do not ask me.'
Then I fainted. Poor Clerval! I was very ill for several months.
Henry nursed me. He did not tell my family how ill I was. He   55
did not wish to worry them.

Slowly I recovered. By the time I was well enough to look
out of my window again, it was springtime. One morning,
Henry brought me a letter. It was from Elizabeth.

1 **After reading to the end, tick the correct answers following the statements below.**

1. Victor collected his instruments:
   a. to go away
   b. to give life to the dead body
   c. to move to another room

2. Victor realized that the creature was:
   a. beautiful
   b. watery
   c. monstrous

3. Victor ran out of the room because:
   a. he was tired
   b. he was horrified
   c. he was hungry

4. In Victor's dream Elizabeth appeared:
   a. crawling in the shroud folds
   b. very beautiful
   c. pale and cold

5. When Victor woke up his forehead was:
   a. dry
   b. red
   c. cold with sweat

6. Victor spent the night outside because:
   a. he wanted to go for a walk
   b. the monster was following him
   c. the creature had tried to touch him

7. The next morning Victor met:
   a. Clerval
   b. his father
   c. Elizabeth

8. Victor's family was:
   a. healthy
   b. worried
   c. quite happy

9. Clerval realized that Victor was ill because he looked:
   a. unhappy
   b. thin and pale
   c. healthy

10. When Victor returned home, he realized that:
    a. the house was empty
    b. the house was crowded
    c. everyone had fainted

11. After a period of sickness Victor received:
    a. a letter from his father
    b. some nice presents
    c. a letter from Elizabeth

Chapter Four

My dear Victor,
We are so worried about you. I know you cannot
write yet, but please write to us as soon as you
can. Get well soon and come home to us. You will
find a happy home full of people who love you.   5
Your father is in good health. William has grown
tall. He is a lovely little boy, with his smiling blue
eyes. Justine, the servant who nursed your mother
during her last illness, has returned to us after an
unhappy time with her own family. Poor Justine!   10
I think she loves us as if we were her real family.
I know that she loved your mother very much.
    Get better soon, dear Victor, and please write to us.
Thank Henry for his kindness and his many letters.
                              Your affectionate   15
                                    Elizabeth

Frankenstein's Narrative

I wrote to my family that day. As soon as I was well enough, I took Clerval to meet the professors at the university.

I did not return to my studies. The thought of science filled me with anxiety and disgust. Instead, I read poetry and studied Oriental languages with Clerval. I stayed with him in Ingolstadt all that year. When spring arrived again, Henry and I went for walks together in the countryside. The blue sky and green fields made me very happy. I made plans to visit my family.

One Sunday, I returned from our walk to find a letter waiting for me.

Chapter Five

The letter was from my father.

My dear Victor,
How can I tell you what has happened? We were
all so happy, waiting for you to come home. I want
to prepare you for the awful news, but it is 5
impossible.
William is dead! Your sweet little brother has
been murdered! Last Thursday, Elizabeth,
William, and I went for a walk in Plainpalais.
William ran off to play. When it came time to go 10
home, we called his name, but he did not answer.
We searched until it was dark, but we could not

Frankenstein's Narrative

find him. Then Elizabeth said he might have gone home. We returned to the house, but he was not there. We went back to Plainpalais with torches and servants to help in the search. About five o'clock in the morning, I found him, dead. The marks of the murderer's fingers were on his neck.

When Elizabeth saw the body, she cried, 'Oh, God! I have murdered my lovely boy!' She told me that she had given William a locket[1] on a chain with a picture of your mother inside it. The locket is gone. Perhaps the murderer killed William for the locket.

Come home, dear Victor! We need you. Do not think of revenge. Just come home to those who love you.

Your father,
Alphonse Frankenstein
Geneva, 12 May 17—

1. **locket** : a piece of jewellery usually containing a picture, which a woman wears around her neck.

Chapter Five

Horrified by this news, I said goodbye to Clerval and left for Geneva immediately. At first I wished to get home as soon as possible, to comfort my poor family, but when I got close to Geneva I began to feel afraid. I stopped two days at Lausanne, in a state of nervous anxiety. Then the lake and the mountains calmed me, and I continued my journey.

The sight of Mont Blanc brought tears to my eyes. As I approached my home town I became afraid again. It was dark when I arrived, and the city gates were already closed for the night. I decided to visit the place where William had died and spend the night in a nearby village. When I got to Plainpalais, there was a thunderstorm. I watched the lightning over Mont Blanc.

Suddenly, in a flash of lightning, I saw a gigantic figure nearby. It was the monster! Was he the murderer of my little brother? I began to tremble. In another flash of lightning I saw him climbing Mont Salêve with amazing speed. He soon reached the top and disappeared.

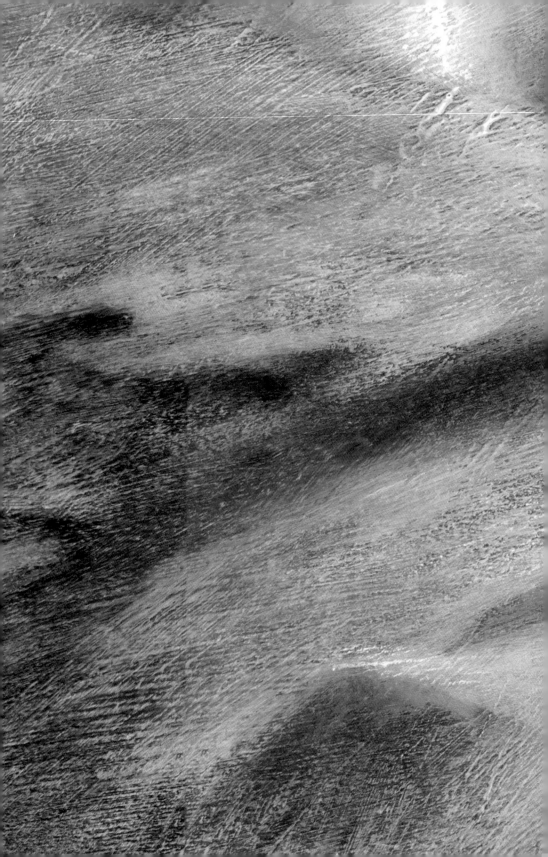

Frankenstein's Narrative

Two years had passed since I created the monster. Was this his first crime? I spent the rest of the night in the mountains, trembling and crying. I felt as if the monster were a horrible part of myself, forced to destroy everyone I loved.

60   The sun rose, and I hurried to my father's house. I wanted to tell what I knew of the murderer, but then I thought, 'If I tell the truth, everyone will think I am mad.' I decided to remain silent.

    My father and Elizabeth met me at the door. They were
65 both thin and pale with sorrow. [1]

---

  1. **sorrow** : great sadness.

Chapter Five

'Welcome, my dearest Victor,' said my father. 'What a pity you did not come months ago, when we were happy. Poor William! He was such a lovely, little boy!'

We three all wept [1] in each other's arms. Then my father said, 'It makes me even sadder to think that Justine could have done such a thing.'

'Justine?' I asked, amazed.

'Did you not know?' asked Elizabeth. 'Justine has been arrested for the murder of William.'

'But she is innocent,' I said.

'I wish I could believe that,' said my father. He explained that on the morning after the murder Justine had fallen ill and spent several days in bed. One of the servants, taking Justine's clothes to be washed, found something in her pocket. It was the locket, with the picture of my mother inside, that had been on a chain around William's neck.

'Justine is innocent,' I said again.

'Oh thank you, Victor,' cried Elizabeth. 'I feel sure that she is innocent. Perhaps you can prove it. You are so kind and generous. No one else believes in poor Justine.'

---

1. **wept** : cried.

1 Look back at Chapters 4 and 5 and complete the following sentences.

1. **Elizabeth's letter.**

   a. .... was worried about Victor.

   b. .... is in good health.

   c. .... has grown tall.

   d. .... has come back home.

2. **Alphonse Frankenstein's letter.**

   a. The family was waiting for ....

   b. William was ....

   c. Last Thursday Elizabeth, William and Alphonse went
      ....

   d. William ran off to ....

   e. When it was time to return home ....

   f. They thought that William had gone ....

   g. William was found dead at ....

   h. The marks of the murderer's ....

   i. The locket with the picture of William's
      mother ....

   j. Victor is asked not to think of ....

2 **Answer the following questions by using short answers. Then justify all your no-answers.**

Ex: Was Justine feeling sick? Yes, she was.

a. Did Victor leave for Geneva immediately?

....

b. Did Victor feel afraid while approaching Geneva?

....

c. Did Victor cry at seeing Mont Blanc?

....

d. Was it morning when Victor reached his town?

....

e. Was the weather nice when Victor got to Plainpalais?

....

f. Was the monster there too?

....

g. Had 20 years passed since Victor's creation of the monster?

....

h. Did Victor confess what he knew about the murderer?

....

i. Was Victor received by Elizabeth only?

....

j. Did Justine feel well after William's death?

....

k. Was the locket found in Justine's dirty clothes?

....

l. Did Elizabeth believe in Justine's innocence?

....

Chapter Six

At eleven o'clock Justine's trial began. In the court I suffered torture. Was I to be the cause of her death too? I wanted to tell everyone that I was the guilty one, but I had not been in Geneva at the time. Everyone would think I was mad, and Justine would be punished anyway.

She told her story to the court. 'I went to search for William,' she said. 'I searched for hours. It was late at night, and I was tired. I lay down in a barn [1] to rest for a few minutes, but then I fell asleep. In the morning, I woke up feeling ill, so I went home and went to bed. I do not know how

1. **barn** : farm building.

Chapter Six

the locket, with the picture of Mrs Frankenstein inside, came to be in my pocket.'

They did not believe her. Justine was found guilty of the murder. I felt sick with horror and despair. The next day 15 she was hanged. Elizabeth wept, but her sadness was the sadness of innocence. I, the true murderer, had no hope or comfort.

Chapter Seven

I felt as if my soul were in hell. I wanted to kill the monster I had created. When I thought of him, my mind was full of hatred and revenge. I wished to see him again so that I could avenge the deaths of William and Justine.

My father became ill with sadness and grief. Elizabeth grew pale and thin. I felt horribly guilty. My only comfort was to escape to the mountains and forget my sorrows for a few days. The mountains and rivers were made by God. In the magnificent Alpine valleys, I felt His power and was afraid of nothing else.

On one of these journeys, in August, nearly two years after the death of Justine, I entered the valley of Chamonix. Rivers of ice came down from the mountains. The great white dome of Mont Blanc stood above me. I decided to climb Montanvert. I remembered the view from the top of the mountain. That sublime landscape alone could tranquillize my soul.

1 **Scan through Chapters 6 and 7 and complete this table.**

Starting time of Justine's trial	
How Victor felt	
Why Victor did not speak	
What Justine told the court	
How the trial ended	
Victor's reaction	
Why Victor wanted to see the monster	

2 **Answer:**

What happened to Victor's father?

Where could Victor feel better two years later?

....

....

....

....

....

Before reading

1 How do you feel when it is sunny? How do you feel when it is rainy?

How do you feel in front of a beautiful landscape on a sunny day?
Do you think that both the weather and nature condition your mood?
Compare/contrast your answers with your classmates.

2 While listening to the first part of Chapter 8 (lines 1-13) complete
the following grid:

Place	
Who	
Description of the setting	
Character's feelings	

Now read and check your answers.

Chapter Eight

 ontanvert is very steep. The path winds slowly up the mountain. The pine trees on both sides were heavy with snow. It was midday when I arrived at the top of the mountain. Then I climbed down onto the glacier. I spent two hours crossing that great river of ice. Then I sat on a rock to rest, looking back at Montanvert and, behind it, Mont Blanc. The snowy peaks of the mountains glistened [1] above the clouds in the sunshine. For a moment I was happy.

5

10

---

1. **glistened** : shone brightly.

Frankenstein's Narrative

Suddenly I saw a man running towards me over the ice. As he approached me at great speed, I recognized him. It was the monster I had created! I trembled with hatred and anger. 'Devil!' I cried. 'Are you not afraid to approach me? Are you not afraid that I will avenge the deaths of those you have murdered?'

'I expected this,' said the monster. 'Everyone hates me. I am the most miserable creature on earth. Even you, my creator, hate me. You say you will kill me. How dare you play with life and death! Do your duty towards me, and I will do my duty towards you and the rest of mankind. [1] Do what I ask and I will leave you and them in peace. If you refuse, I will murder everyone you love.'

'Hateful monster! Devil! I was mad to create you. Now I will destroy you!'

'Be calm,' he said, 'and hear my story. Remember that you made me stronger than you. Oh Frankenstein, you are fair to everyone else! Be fair to me, your creature, as well! I should be your Adam, but instead I am your Satan. Everywhere I see happiness, but for me there is no happiness. I was good, but unhappiness made me evil. [2] Make me happy, and I will be

1. **mankind** : the human race.
2. **evil** : morally bad.

Chapter Eight

good again.'

'Go!' I cried. 'I will not listen to you. We are enemies. Either go or fight with me until one of us is dead.'

'How can I make you understand?' replied the monster. 35
'I was capable of love and kindness. But I am alone. Everyone hates me. I hide in the mountains. I live in the caves of ice. If people knew of my existence, they would try to kill me. How can I love them when they hate me? If I am unhappy, I will make them unhappy too, but you can save them. If you refuse 40 my request, I will kill not only you and your family but many others too. Listen to my tale. In court, the guilty are allowed to speak in their own defence before they are condemned. You say I am a murderer, but you want to murder me, your own creature. Listen to me, and then, if you wish, destroy the work 45 of your own hands.'

'Do not remind me that I am your creator. I wish you had never come to life. I curse my own hands for having made you! Go! I hate the sight of you!'

'Then do not look at me,' said the monster, and he put his 50 horrible hands over my eyes. 'Do not look at me, but listen. Hear my tale; it is long and strange. Before the sun sets this evening, you will know everything. Then you will decide whether I will go away to live a harmless life or stay to murder your fellow creatures.' 55

Frankenstein's Narrative

I agreed to listen to his story. I was curious to know what had happened to him, and, for the first time, I felt that as his creator I had a duty towards him. He took me across the ice to a small hut. Inside, he lit a fire. I sat down, and the monster
60　began his tale.

1 After reading, select the most appropriate word in this multiple-choice summary.

Montanvert was **peaked / covered / heavy** with snow. At midday Victor **went down / descended / climbed** to the glacier. It took Victor **two / three / seven** hours to cross the river of ice. Looking back at Mont Blanc Victor felt **unhappy / happy / very miserable**.

All of a sudden he saw **a mountain / a woman / the monster** running towards him.

The monster said he was **the happiest / the unhappiest / the most scared** creature on earth and asked Victor to **repeat / listen to / read** his story.

The monster added that he had seen **unhappiness / evil / happiness** everywhere and that he had become evil because of his **happiness / unhappiness / sickness**.

Everybody hated him and consequently he had to **die / live / ride** in the caves of ice.

Finally, Victor **agreed / disagreed / went home** to listen to the monster's story and was taken to a small hut where the monster **finished / continued / started** telling his tale.

2 What sort of atmosphere is created in Chapter 8?
What devices does the writer use to create it?
Underline them in the text, then compare your choices with your partner.

3 Would you feel like Victor if you were in the same place?
Why/why not?
How do you react in front of a beautiful woman/man?
Do you think that the appearance of a person conditions or alters his/her acceptance by other people? Think of books you have read or films you have seen on the subject (for example: *The Elephant Man, The Hunchback of Notre Dame, Beauty and the Beast, Dracula, Dr Jekyll and Mr Hyde,...*). Discuss your answers with your classmates.

Before reading

1 Read the following sentences, then listen to lines 1-35 and put them in the correct order. The first has been done for you.

☐ The monster ate berries and drank river-water.

☐ The monster took Victor's coat because he was cold.

1 The monster did not remember the beginning of his life.

☐ The monster found shelter in the forest.

☐ The monster woke up at night and was afraid.

☐ The monster collected some wood to light a fire.

☐ The monster felt happy at hearing the birds singing.

2 What do you expect will happen to the monster?
Discuss your predictions with your classmates.

Chapter Nine

The Monster's Narrative

I do not remember very much about the beginning of my life. I saw, felt, heard, and smelt all at the same time. When I left your apartment, I took your coat, because I was cold. I remember the light grew strong, and I had to close my eyes. I looked for shade [1] and found it in the forest of Ingolstadt. There I rested by a river. After a while I felt hungry and thirsty. I drank from the river and ate some berries, then I fell asleep.

5

---

1. **shade** : shelter/protection from sunlight.

The Monster's Narrative

10   'When I awoke it was dark and cold. I was frightened. I sat down and wept. Soon a gentle light came, and I saw a shining white form rise above the trees. I felt only hunger and thirst and light and darkness. When I looked at the moon I felt pleasure.

15   'Days and nights passed. Slowly I began to distinguish the things around me. I discovered that the pleasant sounds I often heard came from the birds that flew across the light. That pleased me. Sometimes I tried to imitate their sounds, but I could not.

20   'The moon disappeared from the night. Then it came again, but smaller this time. I was still in the forest. One cold day I found a fire that some travellers had left burning. The warmth of the fire gave me pleasure. I put my hand into the fire and felt pain. Crying and nursing my hand, I looked at the fire. How strange, I thought, that it gives both pleasure and pain. I saw that it was made of wood. I gathered wood to keep the fire burning, then

Chapter Nine

lay down beside it to sleep.
35

'Often I spent the whole day looking for food. Sometimes I went to sleep hungry. I decided to leave the forest and find another place where there was more food. I began my journey in the evening and walked for three days. Then I came to the open country. Snow had fallen the night before, and the fields 40 were white. I shivered with cold. In the morning I saw a small hut. I entered. Inside was an old man, preparing some food over a fire. When he saw me, he screamed and ran out of the hut. He ran across the fields and disappeared from sight. I had never seen a hut before, and it seemed a wonderful place. I ate the old 55 man's food then lay down and fell asleep.

'I awoke at midday and continued my journey. At sunset I arrived at a village. I admired the huts and cottages. I saw vegetables growing in the gardens. I saw milk and cheese

The Monster's Narrative

60 through the windows of the cottages. I was hungry. When I
entered a cottage, the children inside screamed, and a woman
fainted. The villagers [1] came running. Some attacked me.
I escaped to the open country. I hid myself in a small hut
beside a cottage. It was bare and uncomfortable, but I was

65 happy to have found a place to hide from the weather and
from the violence of human beings.

'Lying in the hut, looking out through a crack [2] in its
wooden wall, I saw a young woman. She carried a
bucket filled with milk. She looked sad. Then a
young man appeared. He too had a sad expression.
He took the bucket from her and carried it into
the cottage. She followed, and they
disappeared from sight.

'My hut shared one wall with their cottage.
In this wall there was a window, but it was
covered with planks [3] of wood. One of the
planks had a small hole in it. I looked
through the hole. The inside of their
cottage was clean but very bare. An old
man sat beside the fire, playing a musical

---

1. **villagers** : people who live in a village.
2. **crack** : narrow opening.
3. **planks** : long, narrow pieces of wood.

Chapter Nine

instrument. The sound he made was more beautiful than the sounds of birds. The young woman was sitting close to him. I could see that there were tears in her eyes. The old man did not notice this until she sobbed [1] aloud. Then he called her name. She came to him, and he put his arms around her. I felt both pleasure and pain watching them. I had never felt that way before, and I moved away from the window, unable to bear my emotions.

'When night came, I was surprised to see that the cottagers [2] could make light with candles. They sat around the fire, and the young man made sounds that I did not understand. I now know he was reading aloud to them. After a while, they put out the candles and went to bed.'

1. **sobbed** : cried.
2. **cottagers** : people who live in a cottage.

1 **Look back at Chapter 9 and say**

WHY

a. The monster decided to leave the forest.

b. The fields were white.

c. The man inside the hut shouted.

d. The monster was attacked by the villagers.

e. The monster felt happy in the small hut near the cottage.

f. The monster was able to see the people in the house.

2 **Refer to lines 67-81 and complete the following table:**

What were the cottagers doing when the monster looked at them through the crack in the wall?

The young woman	
The young man	
The old man	

Chapter Ten

I lay on the floor of my hut, but I could not sleep. I thought about the cottagers. How kind and gentle they were! I longed to be with them, but I was afraid. I remembered how the villagers had attacked me. I decided to stay quietly in my hut, watching the gentle cottagers through the hole in the window.

'I soon discovered that the old man was blind. He spent his days sitting by the fire. Sometimes he played music. The young man and the young woman were very gentle and kind to him. At first I thought that their lives must be happy. They had food, fire, and friendship with each other. Yet I noticed that all three looked sad. It was a long time before I discovered that they were very poor. Sometimes in the winter

The Monster's Narrative

there was very little to eat. On those days, the young woman
15　put all the food on the old man's plate, and she and her
brother ate nothing.

　'Slowly I realized that they could communicate with each
other by making sounds. This was really a godlike [1] science!
I wanted very much to learn to speak, but it was difficult.
20　After a few months in my hut, listening to them, I could say
'fire', 'milk', 'food', and 'wood'. I also learned the people's
names. The young woman was called 'sister' or 'Agatha'. The
young man was called 'Felix', 'brother', or 'son'. But the old
man had only one name, 'father'. I was very happy each time
25　I learned a new word. Some words, like 'good', 'dearest', and
'unhappy', I heard but did not understand.

'I spent the winter listening to them
and learning. I hid in the hut during
the day and came
out at night to
look for food. I
also collected
fire wood
and left it
for the
cottagers.

1.　**godlike** : like the gods; divine.

Chapter Ten

Sometimes I swept the snow [1] from their path. In the morning, when they found the wood and the clean path, they were very surprised. They spoke to each other, using words like 'good spirit' and 'wonderful', but I did not yet understand those words.

40

'Every evening Felix read aloud to the others. At first I did not understand what he was doing. Then I realized that he used many of the same sounds in his reading as he used in speech. I thought perhaps there were signs for words written on the paper. I wanted very much to learn to read those signs.

'I knew that I could not show myself to the cottagers until I had mastered [2] their language. Maybe my words could win their sympathy, despite my monstrous appearance. My cottagers were graceful and beautiful. I loved to look at them, but how frightened I was the first time I saw my face reflected

55

---

1. **swept the snow** : cleaned with a brush.
2. **mastered** : learned well.

in the water! At first I could not believe that it was my own
60   face. When I realized that the horrible reflection really was
me, I felt great sadness and shame.

'Spring arrived. The air was warm, birds sang, and leaves
began to grow on the trees. Happy, happy earth! Everything
was so green and beautiful that I was filled with joy. I spent
65   many hours imagining the future. In these fantasies, I showed
myself to the cottagers. At first they were horrified by my
appearance, but then I slowly persuaded them to accept me
and even to love me.'

1 After reading the chapter carefully, complete these sentences using the words in the cottage:

a. The cottagers were ....

b. The monster was .... to show himself to them.

c. The old man was ....

d. The young man and woman were .... to the old man.

e. The cottagers looked sad because they were ....

f. It was .... for the monster to learn to speak.

g. The monster felt .... when he learnt a new word.

h. The cottagers were .... when they found some wood.

i. The monster was very .... when he saw his face in the water.

j. In spring the monster was filled with .... because everything was .... and ....

2 The cottagers are 'kind' and 'gentle'. What do you think their reaction will be when meeting the monster?

Before reading

1 Match these parts of sentences as appropriate. Then listen to the first paragraph and check your answers.

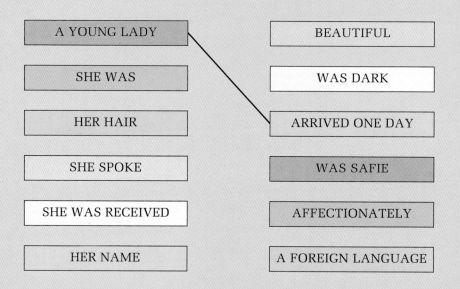

Chapter Eleven

ne day in the spring a young lady arrived at the cottage. As soon as he saw her, Felix's expression changed from sadness to great joy. When the young lady spoke to the cottagers, they did not understand her. ⁵ It seemed she had a language of her own. She was very beautiful, with dark hair and eyes. Felix called her his 'sweet Arabian'. She did not understand but smiled. The old man embraced the young stranger affectionately. Gentle Agatha kissed her hands. ¹⁰

'In the evening I noticed that the cottagers were repeating the same sounds again and again. The young stranger repeated after them. I realized that they were teaching her their

The Monster's Narrative

language. If I listened, I too could learn. When the stranger
went to bed, Felix said, 'Goodnight, sweet Safie.'

'The days passed peacefully. The only difference was that
now my cottagers were happy instead of sad. Safie and I
learned the language very quickly. Meanwhile, the woods
were full of flowers, and the nights grew warm and pleasant.

'My days were spent in study. I learned more quickly than
Safie. We learned to read as well as to speak. The book Felix
used to teach Safie was Volney's *Ruins of Empires*. Felix
explained everything as he read aloud. Through this book I
learned a little about
the histories,
governments,
customs, and
religions of
many
different
countries.
I heard of
the Greeks
and early
Romans.
I heard of the decline
of the Roman Empire, chivalry,
Christianity, and kings. I heard of the

Chapter Eleven

discovery of America and wept with Safie over the sad fate of
the American Indians.

'These stories amazed me. How could human beings be so
powerful, noble, and good, but, at the same time, so violent
and evil? I learned of the division of property, the rich and the
poor, and of aristocratic families.

'I learned that to be rich and from an aristocratic family
was the best condition. A person could be respected with only
one of these advantages, but with neither of them he was a
slave. He had to work for the good of the fortunate few.

'And what was I? I knew nothing of my creator. I had no
money, no friends, and no property, and I was horribly ugly.
I was not even a human being. I saw and heard of no others
like me. The smiles of Safie and the gentle words of Agatha
were not for me. I was a monster, alone in the world. My
sadness grew with my knowledge. I wished that I had stayed
in the woods and never known anything more than hunger,
thirst, and cold.'

1 **Look back at Chapter 11 and then answer the following questions:**

   a. What did the monster learn from *Ruins of Empires*?

   b. Why was the monster amazed by the stories?

   c. Why did the monster say: 'My sadness grew with my knowledge'?

Before reading

1 **While listening to Chapter 12 decide whether the following sentences are true or false. Tick (✔) the correct column.**

		True	False
a.	The old man's name was De Lacey.	☐	☐
b.	Safie's father was imprisoned and sentenced to death.	☐	☐
c.	Felix did not help Safie's father.	☐	☐
d.	Safie could not speak French.	☐	☐
e.	Safie's mother taught her to be a Christian.	☐	☐
f.	Safie wanted to live in a harem.	☐	☐
g.	Safie and her father left Paris under false names.	☐	☐
h.	De Lacey and Agatha were arrested in Germany.	☐	☐
i.	Safie obeyed her father's orders.	☐	☐

Check your answers by reading the text.

Chapter Twelve

Slowly I came to understand the history of my cottagers. The old man's name was De Lacey. He was a Frenchman of good family. They had lived in Paris in a beautiful house. Safie's father was a Turkish merchant who had lived in Paris for many years. On the day Safie arrived from Constantinople to live with him, her father was put in prison by the French government for some crime I did not understand. Many people felt that he had been unjustly condemned. Felix was present in the court when the Turk was condemned to death. Horrified, Felix decided to help him to escape from prison. The Turk offered money, but Felix refused to take it. Then he saw the lovely Safie, and he fell in love with her.

The Monster's Narrative

'In the days before the escape, Safie wrote several letters to
Felix, with the help of a servant who understood French.
I have copies of these letters, which I will give to you. They
will prove that my story is true. In her letters, Safie explained
that her mother was a Christian Arab who had been enslaved [1]
by the Turks. Safie's father fell in love with her and married
her. Her mother, born in freedom, taught Safie to be a
Christian and to want more liberty than Muslim women are
allowed. Although her mother was dead, Safie remembered
these things. She did not want to return to Asia and live in a
harem. She wanted to marry a Christian and live in a Christian
country.

'On the day of the escape, old De Lacey and Agatha left
their house and hid in an obscure part of Paris. Felix,
meanwhile, left Paris with the Turk and Safie, who were
travelling on passports in the names of old De Lacey and
Agatha. They left France and travelled through Italy. Safie's
father wished to return to Turkey. He promised Safie and
Felix that they would be married, but secretly he hated the
idea of his daughter marrying a Christian.

'News came from Paris that old De Lacey and Agatha had
been arrested and put in prison for helping the Turk to escape.

---

1. **enslaved** : made a slave.

Chapter Twelve

Felix immediately went back to Paris. The Turk agreed to leave Safie in a convent in Leghorn, where Felix could find her when he returned. Felix and his family were put on trial and found guilty. They lost their fortune and were exiled from France. [1] Felix wrote to the Turk to tell of his misfortunes and his new home in Germany, but the Turk had not kept his promise. He had returned to Turkey, ordering Safie to follow with his property when it arrived in Leghorn. Safie tried to argue with him, but he left in anger, ordering her again to follow him in a few days. Once alone, Safie sold her jewels and travelled with a servant to Germany to find Felix and his family.'

40

---

1. **exiled from France** : forced to leave France.

Before reading

 1 Work with a partner and try to fill in the following gapped text using the words in the box below.

> *hut   condition   peacefully   death*
> *from   cottagers   bag   ugly   feeling*
> *life   to love   August   happiness*
> *human   sadness   different*

One night in ...., when I was walking in the woods, I found a .... full of books. I took it and ran back to my .... The books were *Paradise Lost*, Plutarch's *Lives,* *and The Sorrows of Werther*. These treasures gave me great .... They showed me new worlds of thought and .... Sometimes they filled me with joy, but more often they filled me with .... I thought Werther a divine being, and I wept at his ...., although I did not really understand it.

As I read, I thought of my own feelings and .... In some ways I resembled the people in these books, but in other ways I was .... from them. I was alone. My body was gigantic and .... What did this mean? Who was I? What was I? Where did I come ....? What was the purpose of my .... ? I asked myself these questions often, but I could not answer them.

Plutarch's *Lives* taught me .... and admire the heroes of the past. I read about men who governed or murdered their fellow .... beings. I preferred those who governed ...., because they resembled my ....

Check your answers by listening to the cassette.

Chapter Thirteen

One night in August, when I was walking in the woods, I found a bag full of books. I took it and ran back to my hut. The books were *Paradise Lost*, Plutarch's *Lives*, and *The Sorrows of Werther*. These treasures 5 gave me great happiness. They showed me new worlds of thought and feeling. Sometimes they filled me with joy, but more often they filled me with sadness. I thought Werther a divine being, and I wept at his death, although I did not really understand it. 10

'As I read, I thought of my own feelings and condition. In some ways I resembled ¹ the people in these books, but in

---

1. **resembled** : was similar to.

other ways I was different from them. I was alone. My body was gigantic and ugly. What did this mean? Who was I? What

15 was I? Where did I come from? What was the purpose of my life? I asked myself these questions often, but I could not answer them.

'Plutarch's *Lives* taught me to love and admire the heroes of the past. I read about men who governed or murdered their

20 fellow human beings. I preferred those who governed peacefully, because they resembled my cottagers.

'When I read *Paradise Lost,* I thought it was a true story. It often reminded me of my own condition. Like Adam, I was the only example of my kind, but God made Adam beautiful.

25 Adam's creator cared for him and talked to him. I was completely alone. Often I thought I resembled Satan more than Adam. Like Satan, I saw the happiness of other creatures, and I felt envious.

'The coat I took from your apartment had some papers in the pocket. When I had learned to read, I looked at them.

Chapter Thirteen

They were your journal for the four months before you created
me. When I read it, I cursed my creator. [1] Why did you make
me so horribly ugly that even you turned from me in disgust?   40
Even Satan had friends, the other devils, to admire him, but
I had nobody. My creator had abandoned me.

'The autumn passed. I saw, with
surprise and grief, the leaves fall
from the trees. Nature became
once again cold and sad,
as it was when I first
awoke in the woods. In
summer the flowers and
birds had comforted me.
Now I longed even more to
show myself to the cottagers.
To win their affection was my
greatest ambition.

'I decided to enter the cottage
when the old man was alone.
I knew that my ugliness frightened people, but my voice was
not frightening. I thought that I could talk to the old man first
and win his sympathy.

'One day in winter Safie, Agatha, and Felix went for a walk   60

---

1. **cursed my creator** : wished misfortune on my creator.

87

The Monster's Narrative

in the countryside. The old man was left alone in the cottage. Trembling with excitement and fear, I knocked on the door of the cottage.

'"Who is there?" said the old man. "Come in."

65 '"I am sorry to disturb you," I said. "I am a traveller, and I am tired. Please would you let me sit by your fire for a few minutes?"

'"Come in," said the old man. "My children are not home, and I am blind, so I will not be able to get you food."

70 '"I have food. All I need is a little warmth."

'I sat down. After a silence, the old man asked, "Are you French?"

'"No," I replied, "but I was educated by a French family. I am going to some friends who, I hope, will help me."

75 '"Are they German?" asked the old man.

'"No. They are French. I have no other friends in the world. These people have never seen me, and I am afraid, because if they will not help me I have no other hope."

'"Do not despair. If your friends are good people, they will
80 help you."

'"They are kind," I said. "They are wonderful people, but they are prejudiced against me. I am not bad. I have never hurt anyone, but when they look at me they will see a horrible monster."

Chapter Thirteen

'"If you really mean no harm,[1] can you not explain that to
them?"

'"Yes. I will try. I love these friends very much. For many
months I have been doing small things to help them, but they
believe I want to hurt them."

'"Where do they live?" asked the old man.

'"Nearby."

'"If you will tell me your story, perhaps I can help you. I
cannot see your face, but I like your voice. I want to help you."

'"Thank you!" I cried. "Those are the first kind words that
have ever been spoken to me."

'"Will you tell me the names of your friends?" he asked.

'At that moment I heard the sounds of the young people
returning to the cottage. "Help me!" I cried. "Now is the
moment! You and your family are the friends for whom I am
searching. Do not abandon me!"

'Felix, Safie, and Agatha entered the cottage. How can I
describe their horror when they saw me? Agatha fainted. Safie
ran out of the cottage. Felix attacked me and hit me with a
stick. I could have killed him with my bare hands, but I did
not. Filled with pain and sorrow, I ran out of the cottage and
escaped unseen to my hut.'

---

1. **mean no harm** : have no intention to hurt.

1 Look back at Chapter 13 and select the most appropriate word in this multiple-choice summary:

When the monster read *Paradise Lost* he   ***did not think / thought***
it was a real story. He   ***felt / did not feel***   as beautiful as Adam and
envied the happy condition of all other creatures.

When he had learnt how to read he could understand what was
written on Victor's journal and he   ***blessed / cursed***   his creator.
He realized he   ***was not / was***   alone.

In   ***winter / summer***   he decided to   ***meet / kill***   the cottagers.
He   ***spoke / didn't speak***   to the old man first and   ***told / said***   him
that he looked horrible. When Safie, Felix and Agatha arrived the
monster was hit with a   ***stone / stick***   and   ***ran away / fainted***.

Chapter Fourteen

ursed creator! Why did I live? Why did I not die in that horrible moment? I felt angry, and I wanted revenge. I could have destroyed the cottage and killed the cottagers with pleasure. When night came, I left the hut and ran howling through the woods. The cold stars shone down on me, and the bare trees swayed in the wind. Like Satan, I carried a hell inside me. From that moment I was at war with mankind, and above all, with the man who had given me this miserable life.

'When I returned to the cottage, I found that the cottagers had left. I waited all day. They did not return. That night in anger I placed wood around the cottage and set fire to it. The

cottage burned quickly to the ground, and I ran into the
15 woods.

'Where could I go? I thought of you. I knew from your
journal that you were my father, my creator, and that Geneva
was your home town. I decided to go there. You were my only

hope, but I hated you.

'It was a long and difficult
journey. Because I was
afraid of being seen by
human beings, I travelled
only at night. Rain and
snow fell upon me. I had
nowhere to hide. As I came
closer to your home town,
my anger and my desire for
revenge grew stronger.

'One morning I continued
walking after the sun had
risen. The forest was far

from any village, so I thought I was safe. It was the beginning
of spring. The sun warmed me, and I felt happy for the first
35 time in many months. Walking by the side of a river, I heard
human voices. I hid myself under a tree. A young woman ran
towards the place where I was hidden. Suddenly, she slipped
and fell into the river. I ran out of my hiding place and

The Monster's Narrative

jumped into the river to save her. When I carried her onto the
40   river bank, she fainted. Then a man appeared. He ran towards
me and took the young woman from my arms. Then he turned
and ran into the forest. I followed him. When the man saw me
behind him, he shot me with a gun. I fell to the ground, and
he escaped into the woods.

45   'I was in awful pain. Was this the reward for my kindness?
I had saved a human being from death, and now I suffered for
it. I swore revenge on all mankind. For several weeks I lived a
miserable life in the forest, trying to nurse my wound. Finally
it healed, [1] and I continued my journey.

50   'It was evening when I reached the countryside around
Geneva. I was very tired and lay down to sleep in a field.
I was woken by the approach of a beautiful child. As I looked
at him, I thought perhaps he was too young to be frightened of
me. If I could take him with me and educate him, I would not
55   be alone anymore. I tried to take him in my arms, but when he
saw me he put his hands over his face and screamed.

    '"Why are you screaming, child?" I said. "I will not hurt
you."

    '"Let me go!" cried the child. "Monster! Ugly monster! You
60   want to kill me and eat me! Let me go, or I will tell my father!"

---

1. **healed** : became healthy and normal again.

Chapter Fourteen

'"Come with me," I said.

'"No!" cried the boy. "Let me go! My father is Mr Frankenstein, the magistrate. He will punish you."

'"Frankenstein!" I cried. "Then you are from the family of my enemy."
65

'The child kept screaming at me. I put my hands around his throat to silence him. The next moment he lay dead at my feet.

'I looked at the dead child, and I felt glad. "I too can cause pain," I thought. "This will make Frankenstein suffer!"

'Then I saw something around his neck. It was a chain and
70
locket. In the locket was a picture of a lovely woman. For a few moments I looked at it with pleasure, then my anger returned. No woman would ever love me. If this woman could see me she would faint or scream.

'I left the place where I had murdered the child to look for a hiding place. I entered a barn. There I found a
80
young woman asleep. She was not as beautiful as the woman in the picture, but she was young and healthy. "She will smile at everyone except for me," I thought. I bent over her and whispered, "Wake up, your lover is here! I would die for one of your smiles. Wake up!"
85

The Monster's Narrative

'She moved in her sleep. I was afraid she would awaken. If she woke up, she would scream, and I would be arrested for the murder. That thought brought out the devil in me. "She, not I, will suffer for the murder," I thought. "It is her fault
90 really, the fault of all the women who will never smile at me." I put the locket in her clothes and ran away.

'After a few days, I came to these mountains. I am alone and miserable. No human being will love me, but someone like myself would love me. Make me a wife, Frankenstein.
95 Create a female of my own kind. This you must do for me.'

1 Look back at Chapter 14 then complete the following sentences using one word only!

a. The monster wished he had ....

b. The monster was at .... with his creator.

c. The monster .... fire to the cottage.

d. The monster decided to go to ....

e. The monster travelled at ....

f. The monster saw a young woman .... into the river.

g. A man shot at the monster with a ....

h. A child woke the monster who was .... in a field near Geneva.

i. After hearing the child's surname the monster .... him.

j. The monster found a .... around the child's neck and took it.

k. The monster went to a .... where a woman was sleeping.

l. The monster put the locket into the woman's ....

m. The monster asked .... to make him a wife.

2 From the episodes of the cottagers and the woman rescued from the river you will have realized that the monster isn't bad, but is looking for friendship and is willing to help people. However, because of his horrible aspect he is considered evil and dangerous in spite of his generosity.
How often are our 'good intentions' misunderstood?
Write about an episode of your life in which your actions/thoughts were misunderstood.

Before reading

While listening to Chapter 15 fill in the blanks.

The monster stopped speaking and waited for an ....
'I refuse to do it,' I said. 'Go away! I have given you your answer.
I will never create another .... like you!'

'You are wrong,' said the monster, 'but instead of being angry, I will
reason with you. I am bad because I am sad. .... hates
me. Why should I pity human beings when they do not pity me? If
.... would be kind to me, I would be kind to them, but
that cannot be. If I cannot have love, I will have .... All
I ask is a female like myself. We will be ...., alone in the
world, but we will have each other. Our lives will not be happy, but
they will be harmless. Do not refuse me.'

I was moved. As his ...., it was my duty to make him
happy if I could. He saw the .... in my expression and
said, 'If you agree, I will go with my wife to the .... of
South America. We can live on berries. We can sleep under the
....'

His words made me pity him, but when I looked at his
.... I felt nothing but disgust. After thinking for a long
time, I said, 'I will do it. You must promise to leave ....
forever as soon as I give you a .... to go with you, and
you must promise to stay away from human beings.'

'I promise!' cried the monster. 'Go home and begin your
.... I will watch you, and when you are ready, I will
appear.'

With these words he left me. I saw him go down the mountain at
great .... He disappeared over the river of ice as the
.... was setting.

2 **Now read the text and check your answers.**

Chapter Fifteen

Frankenstein's Narrative Continues

The monster stopped speaking and waited for an answer. 'I refuse to do it,' I said. 'Go away! I have given you your answer. I will never create another being like you!'

'You are wrong,' said the monster, 'but 5 instead of being angry, I will reason with you. I am bad because I am sad. Everyone hates me. Why should I pity human beings when they do not pity me? If people would be kind to me, I would be kind to them, but that cannot be. If I cannot have love, I will have revenge. All I ask is a female like 10 myself. We will be monsters, alone in the world, but we will

Frankenstein's Narrative Continues

have each other. Our lives will not be happy, but they will be
harmless. Do not refuse me.'

15 I was moved. As his creator, it was my duty to make him
happy if I could. He saw the change in my expression and said,
'If you agree, I will go with my wife to the forests of South
America. We can live on berries. We can sleep under the trees.'

His words made me pity him, but when I looked at his face
I felt nothing but disgust. After thinking for a long time, I
20 said, 'I will do it. You must promise to leave Europe forever as
soon as I give you a female to go with you, and you must
promise to stay away from human beings.'

'I promise!' cried the monster. 'Go home and begin your
work. I will watch you, and when you are ready, I will appear.'

25 With these words he left me. I saw him go down the
mountain at great speed. He disappeared over the river of ice
as the sun was setting.

1 **Match the first half of the sentence with the correct half given below.**

1. If people had been kind to the monster
2. If the monster could not have love
3. If Victor agreed to make a female
4. When the female creature was ready

a. the monster and his wife would go to South America.
b. the monster would appear.
c. he would have been kind to them.
d. he would take revenge.

Chapter Sixteen

I returned to Geneva, but I did not have the courage to begin my horrible work. I was in better health now, and, when I could forget my promise to the monster, I was happier too.

One day my father said to me, 'I am glad to see that you are better, Victor, but I notice that you are still sad sometimes. Is it because of Elizabeth? I have always hoped you and Elizabeth would marry. You have loved each other since you were children, but maybe I have been blind. Perhaps you love Elizabeth as a sister. Perhaps you love someone else and want that other person to be your wife. Am I right, Victor? Is this the reason for your sadness?'

'My dear father,' I replied. 'Do not worry. I love Elizabeth very much, and I want to marry her.'

Chapter Sixteen

'I am so happy to hear that. Why not marry as soon as possible?' 15

The idea of marrying Elizabeth immediately filled me with horror. I had to create the female and see the two monsters leave Europe before I could marry.

An Englishman had made new discoveries in science. I wanted to speak to this man before beginning work on a 20 female for the monster. I thought it would be better to do my awful work in England, far away from my family. Therefore I told my father that I had to go to England and that when I returned I would marry Elizabeth. My father and Elizabeth asked Clerval to travel with me. At first I thought that this 25 would make it more difficult to do my work, but then I was glad. I thought the monster would not come near me while Henry was there. I did not like to leave my family alone, ignorant of their enemy. But I thought that the monster would follow me to England, so my family would be safe. 30

Clerval and I left Geneva in September. On the journey, Clerval noticed all the beauties of nature, but I was gloomy. Slowly his love of nature tranquillized my soul, and I began to enjoy the passing landscape with him.

Clerval, my dear friend! Where is he now? Does he now 35 only exist in my memory? No! His body is gone, but his spirit still visits me!

Forgive me for showing my sorrow. It is so painful to remember him. I will continue my story.

1 **After reading carefully, complete these sentences using the *Past Simple* of an appropriate verb:**

a. Victor .... the courage to start his work.

b. Victor's father .... he was sad sometimes.

c. Victor .... his father that he wanted to marry Elizabeth.

d. Victor .... it would be better to work in England.

e. Victor .... Geneva with Clerval in September.

f. Victor .... the natural landscape while travelling.

2 **Now decide:**

- What the main theme of the chapter is
- How the main theme is dramatically enhanced

3 **What would be the consequences of the creation of a female monster?**
Do you expect that the female monster will actually be created?
Discuss your answers with your partner.

Contextualizing what you are reading:
Sexual Attitudes

In the period in which Mary Shelley lived, the sexual life of human beings was one of the main concerns of middle-class families. Chastity [1] and other virtues were seen as the very foundation of the family. Any infraction of the strict moral rules of the time was punished by expulsion, ostracism [2] or disinheritance. The rules which regarded proper sexual behaviour were not easily followed, and middle-class society more or less tolerated infractions by men who had many chances to have extra-marital affairs with women from the lower classes, and prostitution increased greatly. On the contrary, women had to obey their husbands and had to behave according to a strict code of conduct. It was only at the end of the 19th century that new attitudes towards sexuality in the middle classes began to appear.

Consider what Mary Godwin did when she fell in love with Shelley (refer to the chronology on page 5).
Did she behave according to the current morality?
What do you think were people's reactions?
Discuss your answers with your classmates.

1. **Chastity** : (G.) Keuschheit.
2. **ostracism** : (G.) Ächtung.

Chapter Seventeen

We spent some months in London. Clerval was planning to visit India. He hoped to be able to help the progress of European colonization and trade there. He spoke several of the languages of India and was interested in the people. In London there were many men who could help him.

I spoke to the English scientist, then I began collecting the materials for my creation. I hated the thought of beginning this awful work. After some months, we received a letter from a person in Scotland who invited us to visit him. We left London in March and travelled slowly north. We stayed in Oxford then in Matlock. We spent two months in Cumberland

Chapter Seventeen

and Westmorland, which were almost like the Swiss
mountains. The snow on the northern sides of the mountains,   15
the lakes, and the rivers made us feel at home. Then we went
on to Scotland. I was not sorry. It was now many months since
I had made my promise, and I was afraid of the monster's
disappointment. Sometimes I feared that he might hurt my
family. At other times I thought he would punish me by   20
murdering Clerval. I felt as if I had committed some great
crime.

When we got to Perth in Scotland, I told Clerval that I
wished to travel alone for a month or two. 'Enjoy your visit,'
I told him, 'we will meet here when I return.' Henry did not   25
want me to go. He told me to write to him often and to come
back as soon as possible.

After I left Clerval, I travelled north. I was sure that the
monster had followed me. I went to one of the smallest islands
of Orkney. On the whole island there were only three   30
miserable huts, and one of them was empty. I rented it and
moved in with my instruments and materials. There I worked
every morning. In the evenings I walked by the sea. As my
work proceeded it became more and more hateful to me.
Sometimes I did not work for two or three days. At other times   35
I worked day and night, hoping to finish it quickly. The things
I had to do often made me feel sick, but I continued to work.

1 **Look back at Chapter 17 and complete the following chart:**

How long Victor and Clerval stayed in London	
Why Clerval wanted to go to India	
What they received after some months	
Place/s where Victor and Clerval stayed while going to Scotland	
Why Victor was scared	
Where Victor left Clerval	
Where Victor went	
Why Victor worked day and night	
How Victor felt	

Before reading

 1 **Listen to the first part of Chapter 18 (lines 1-55) and tick the correct answers:**

1. Three years before, Victor:
   a. had begun the thing he was doing
   b. had created a devil
   c. had promised to leave Europe

2. Victor believed that the female creature might:
   a. be horrified by the monster
   b. kiss him
   c. die

3. Victor thought that the monster and his wife might:
   a. live happily
   b. stay in Europe
   c. generate a race of devils

4. Victor destroyed:
   a. the half-finished female creature
   b. the monster
   c. the laboratory

5. The monster:
   a. smiled
   b. killed Victor
   c. ran away

6. From the window Victor saw:
   a. a man in the water
   b. a boat approaching
   c. someone running

7. When Victor's bedroom door opened he saw:
   a. a maid
   b. the monster
   c. the man from the boat

8. The monster threatened Victor that he would:
   a. kill Clerval
   b. kill him
   c. appear on his wedding night

Check your answers by reading the text.

Chapter Eighteen

ne evening I sat in my laboratory. The sun had set, and the moon was rising over the sea. I began to think about what I was doing. 'Three years ago,' I thought, 'I was doing the same thing. I created a devil whose violence has ruined my life. I am now creating another. She might be even more evil than her mate. He has promised to leave Europe and hide himself in the forests of South America, but she has not promised. She might refuse. They might even hate each other. The monster hates the sight of his own face. Might he not hate the sight of his monstrous mate? She might turn from him in disgust. She might leave him.

'If they do leave Europe together,' I thought, 'they will have

Frankenstein's Narrative Continues

children. They will create a race of devils that might destroy
15   mankind. Have I the right, for my own comfort, to do
something that would be a curse on future generations?'
Before, I had been moved by the monster's arguments and
frightened by his threats. Now, for the first time, I realized how
wicked my promise was. I thought with horror that perhaps
20   future generations would curse me as the man whose
selfishness had caused great suffering to the whole of mankind.

I trembled. Then, looking up, I saw the monster at the
window by the light of the moon. He was watching me. His
face was horribly ugly. It was an evil face. Trembling with
25   anger, I tore to pieces the half-finished creature. The monster
saw me destroy his mate. With a howl of pain, he ran away.

I left the room, promising myself that I would never return
to that work. I went to my bedroom and spent hours by my
window, looking out at the moon. There were a few fishing
30   boats on the water. From time to time, the silence was broken
by the voices of the fishermen calling to one another. Then
suddenly I heard the sound of oars in the water. A boat was
approaching the shore. A few minutes later, I heard my front
door open. I trembled with fear and wanted to cry out for
35   help, but I could not. Like someone who is dreaming a
frightening dream, I could neither speak nor move. My
bedroom door opened, and I saw the monster.

He spoke to me in a trembling voice. 'You have destroyed

Chapter Eighteen

the work you began. What does this mean? Will you break
your promise? I have followed you over Europe to this cold   40
gloomy place. I have been tired and hungry, and now you
destroy my hopes.'

'Go away!' I cried. 'Yes, I break my promise. I will never
create another as evil and monstrous as you are.'

'Slave! I reasoned with you before, but you are   45
unreasonable. Remember that I have the power to make you
miserable. You are my creator, but I am your master. Obey!'

'Your threats cannot force me to do something evil,' I said.
'Go away! Your words only make me angrier.'

Frankenstein's Narrative Continues

50   The monster said, 'Every man has a wife. Every animal has
a mate. Will I be the only creature to live alone? I was capable
of love, but everyone hated me. I will not let you be happy
while I am miserable. I want revenge more than warmth or
food. Before I die, you will be sorry that you were ever born.
55 Remember this: I will be with you on your wedding night!'

     He ran away. A few moments later, I saw him in his boat,
which shot [1] across the water with the speed of an arrow. 'So,'
I thought, 'he will murder me on my wedding night.' I thought
of poor Elizabeth. 'How she would suffer if she lost me!'

60   As the sun rose, I went out and walked on the beach. I would
have been happy to live forever on that miserable island, if only
I could live in peace. When I left the island it would be to
meet my own death, or the deaths of those I loved, at the
hands of a monster I myself had created.

65   At midday I fell asleep on the grass. When I awoke, the sun
was setting. What had happened the night before seemed like
a bad dream.

     A fishing boat landed on the beach, and a man from the
boat brought me two letters. One was from my father and the
70 other from Clerval. Clerval wrote that he would soon return to
London to complete the arrangements for his journey to India.
He asked me to meet him at Perth as soon as possible.
I decided to leave the island in two days.

---

1.   **shot** : moved very quickly.

Chapter Eighteen

First I had to pack my chemical instruments. The next morning, I entered my laboratory. The remains of the half-finished creature lay on the floor. I felt almost as if I had murdered a human being. With trembling hands I collected my instruments. Then I gathered the remains of the creature and put them in a basket with some heavy stones.

When the moon rose that night, I went out in a small boat. I felt like a criminal. I waited until a black cloud covered the moon for a few minutes, then I dropped the basket into the sea. Relieved, I lay down in the boat and fell into a deep sleep. 90

When I awoke it was morning. There was a strong wind, and my little boat was in danger. The wind had blown the boat far away from the island, and I did not know where I was. All day the little boat tossed [1] on the sea. I was horribly thirsty and frightened. I thought I was going to die. Then I imagined 95

---

1. **tossed** : moved up and down and side to side.

Frankenstein's Narrative Continues

Elizabeth, my father, and Clerval — all left behind for the monster to murder.

100 At sunset, I saw land in the distance. Tears of joy filled my eyes. As I approached the shore, I saw boats, a harbour, and a small town. I brought my boat into the harbour and stepped onto the shore. People gathered to watch, but they did not offer to help me. 'My friends,' I said, 'could you please tell me
105 the name of this town?'

Nobody replied. The people looked angry and unfriendly. 'What is the matter?' I asked. 'The English are not usually so unfriendly to strangers.'

'I do not know about the English,' said one man, 'but the
110 Irish hate murderers.'

What could this mean? Another man stepped forward and put his hand on my shoulder. 'Come, sir,' he said. 'You must talk to Mr Kirwin.'

'Who is Mr Kirwin? Why must I talk to him?'

115 'He is the magistrate, sir,' said the man. 'He will want to ask you some questions about a gentleman who was found murdered here last night.'

I was surprised but not greatly worried. I was innocent and could prove it. I followed the man to Mr Kirwin's house. I had
120 no idea then of the horror that was waiting for me.

1 Look back at Chapter 18 and complete the sentences below. Then write suitable questions:

a. ....?

Victor .... the monster's boat sailing away quickly.

b. ....?

Victor had a walk on the .... the next morning.

c. ....?

Victor fell .... on the grass at midday.

d. ....?

A man from a boat brought Victor two ....

e. ....?

Because Clerval wanted to arrange everything for his journey to

....

f. ....?

Victor felt like a murderer when he saw the .... of the unfinished creature.

g. ....?

Victor put the creature's remains in ....

h. ....?

Victor left in ....

i. ....?

Victor dropped the basket ....

j. ....?

It was morning when Victor ....

k. ....?

The boat was in danger because ....

2 Scan the text through from line 89 to line 100 and complete the following diagram:

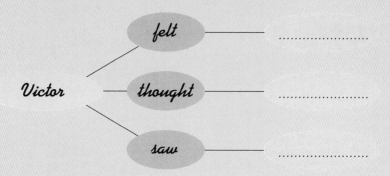

3 What do you expect will happen?
Compare your predictions with your classmates.

4 'Have I the right [...] to do something that would be a curse on future generations?' Frankenstein asks himself.
This is the question that modern scientists also have to face when carrying out experiments in the genetic field. How far do you think scientists should go?
Consider cloning, in vitro fertilization etc.

Chapter Nineteen

 r Kirwin was a kind old gentleman. He asked one of the witnesses to tell his story. The man said he had been fishing the night before with a friend. The wind grew strong, so they landed their 5 boat some distance from the harbour. On the beach they found the body of a young man. There were black finger-marks on his neck.

When I heard about the finger-marks, I began to tremble. The magistrate noticed my nervousness. The other fisherman 10 said that, just before they found the body, he had seen a boat with one man in it not far from the shore. He believed it was the same boat in which I had just landed.

Frankenstein's Narrative Continues

A woman said that she had been standing at the door of her
cottage near the beach, about half an hour before the body was
discovered. She had seen a boat with one man in it leave the
shore near the place where the body was later found.

When Mr Kirwin had heard these witnesses, he took me to
the room where the body lay. I was not worried, because I
knew that I had been seen by people on the island at the time
of the murder. I was sure that I could not be found guilty.

I entered the room. Imagine my horror when I saw on the
table the body of my friend Clerval! 'Oh Henry!' I cried. 'Have
I been the cause of your death too?' I fainted. For two months I
was very ill. They thought I was dying. I cried out in my
illness, calling myself the murderer of William, Justine, and
Henry. Sometimes I begged for help to kill the devil who was
torturing me. At other times I felt his fingers around my neck.
Since I spoke in my own language, only Mr Kirwin understood
me. Why did I not die? What was I made of that I could suffer
so much and still live? In two months I recovered to find
myself in prison. Mr Kirwin was the only person to show me
any kindness. One day he came into my prison cell. 'How are
you?' he asked gently.

'Nothing can comfort me,' I replied.

'When you were ill,' he said, 'I looked at the papers that
were in your pockets. I found a letter from your father, so I
wrote to Geneva to tell him what had happened.'

Chapter Nineteen

'Have you news from my family?' I asked eagerly, 'Has
anything terrible happened?'   40

'Your family is well,' said Mr Kirwin, 'and someone has
come to see you.'

For a moment I thought the monster had come to watch my
suffering. 'Do not let him in!' I cried. 'I cannot see him!'

'Why? Do you not wish to see your father?' asked Mr Kirwin. 45

'My father!' I was weak with relief. 'Oh, please! Where is he?'

Mr Kirwin left the room, and a moment later, my father
entered. I stretched out my hand to him. 'Oh father, you are
safe! And Elizabeth?'

'She is well. Poor Victor! What a terrible place this is! And   50
poor Clerval!'

I wept. 'Yes, my dear father,' I said. 'Some horrible destiny
hangs over me!'

I recovered quickly. After the trial, I was released from prison.
It was proved that I had been on the island at the time of the   55
murder. I travelled home to Geneva with my father, feeling sad
and hopeless. Often I thought of killing myself, but I had a duty
to protect the people I loved from the monster I had created.

Ever since my illness I had taken opium to help me sleep.
The opium gave my body the rest it needed, but my mind still   60
suffered in terrible dreams. Sometimes I dreamt that the
monster's fingers were around my neck. Waking up to find no
monster there, I felt relief. For the moment I was safe.

1 First complete the following questions and then answer the
questions appropriately.

a. .... did Mr Kirwin ask one of the witnesses?

....

b. .... did they find black finger-marks?

....

c. .... had the woman seen a boat with one man?

....

d. .... wasn't Victor worried?

....

e. .... did Victor react in front of Clerval's dead body?

....

f. .... was Victor ill?

....

g. .... was the only person who understood Victor's
language?

....

h. .... had Mr Kirwin found a letter from Victor's father?

....

i. .... did Victor react at hearing that his father was there?

....

j. .... was Victor released?

....

k. .... had Victor taken to help himself to sleep?

....

2 Imagine that you are Victor and write a letter to your father from prison. Include the following points.

- why you are in prison
- how you feel
- what you intend to do.......

You may like to start your letter as follows:

Dear father,

You will never believe what I am about to tell you...

Chapter Twenty

e stopped in Paris for a while, because I
was not strong enough to travel on.
There my father wished me to go out
and see people. He hoped that this
5   would cure my sadness, but I could not
bear to see people. How they would all hate me if they knew
that I had created a monster who took pleasure in murdering
them! In my despair, I told my father more than once that I
was responsible for the deaths of William, Justine, and Henry.
10 Sometimes he asked me to explain. At other times he seemed
to think my words were a result of my illness. I could not
explain. He would have thought I was mad.

A few days before we left Paris, I received a letter from
Elizabeth.

Chapter Twenty

My dear Victor,

I am so glad that you are coming home. How much you must have suffered! I want you to find comfort and tranquillity. For this reason, my dear friend, I am writing to explain something to you.

You know that both your parents always wanted us to get married. We have always loved each other, but perhaps our love is the love of brother and sister. Tell me, dearest Victor. Do you love someone else? You have been away for many years, first in Ingolstadt and then in Britain. When you left last year, I thought maybe you were running away from me. I love you and have always dreamt of a future together with you, but I want your happiness as well as my own. Our marriage would make me miserable if I thought that you did not wish it. Believe me, Victor, I love you too much to make you unhappy. Be happy, my friend. Obey me in this one request, and I will be contented.

Elizabeth
Geneva, 18 May 17—

Frankenstein's Narrative Continues

This letter reminded me of the monster's threat — '*I will be with you on your wedding night.*' On that night the devil would destroy me and so destroy the only hope of happiness I had to comfort me.

40 Sweet Elizabeth! I read her letter several times. I dreamt of the paradise of her love, but the apple was already eaten, and the angel was ready to drive me out of the garden. I decided to marry as soon as I got home. I wrote to tell her this. My letter was calm and affectionate. 'Do not be afraid,

45 my love,' I said. 'My only hope of happiness is in marrying you. I have a terrible secret. When I tell you my secret, you will understand why I have been so miserable. I will tell you on the morning after our wedding. Do not ask me about it until then.'

50 My father was glad. He spoke of the comfort we would be to each other. He spoke of children being born to replace the loved ones we had lost. All I could think of was the monster's threat, '*I will be with you on your wedding night*'. I thought it meant that he would kill me then. I was not afraid of my own

55 death. Great God! If for one moment I had imagined what he really planned to do, I would have left home forever. I thought I was preparing my own death, but really I was preparing hers.

We made the arrangements for the wedding. As the day

60 approached, I began to feel better. The monster's threat

Chapter Twenty

seemed like a bad dream, but my happiness with Elizabeth seemed real and close at hand.

Elizabeth looked a little sad on our wedding day. Perhaps she was thinking of the awful secret I would tell her the next morning. After the wedding, there was a party at my father's house. Then Elizabeth and I left for our honeymoon on Lake Como. Those were the last moments in my life when I felt happiness. The sun was shining. We saw Mont Salêve and, in the distance, Mont Blanc. I held Elizabeth's hand. 'You look sad, Elizabeth,' I said.

'I am content,' she replied. 'Something tells me not to hope for happiness, but I will not listen. Look at the mountains and the lake, Victor. What a divine day! How happy nature appears!'

1 Look back at Chapter 20 and summarise the information included in Elizabeth's letter considering:

- the reason/s why she wrote the letter
- the reason/s why she was worried

2 Look back at page 126-127 and complete:

a. Victor's reactions to Elizabeth's letter:

The letter reminded him of ....

He dreamt of ....

He wrote back to Elizabeth to ....

b. Victor's father's reaction to the news of their marriage:

....

....

c. Victor's feelings at the idea of getting married:

He thought that the monster would ....

He started to feel better as ....

d. Elizabeth's feelings on her wedding day:

....

....

3 After the marriage.
Fill in the blanks with the correct words.

There was a .... at Victor's father's ....
Then Elizabeth and Victor left for .... honeymoon on
.... They saw Mont .... and Mont
.... Elizabeth looked .... to Victor, but she
was ...., because the day was .... and nature
appeared ....

Before reading

1 Listen to Chapter 21 and complete the following grid.

Time	
Weather	
Why Victor did not go to bed at once	
What Victor suddenly heard	
What Victor found in the bedroom	
How Victor reacted	
What Victor found on Elizabeth's neck	
How the monster disappeared	
How Victor's father reacted to the terrible news	
Who Victor told his story to	

Check your answers by reading the text.

Chapter Twenty-one

It was evening when we arrived at the hotel. A strong wind blew from the west. Clouds raced across the moon. It began to rain. I had been calm during the day, but now I was afraid. I kept my hand on the gun in my pocket. Every sound frightened me. 'What is the matter, Victor?' asked Elizabeth.

'Do not ask, my love,' I replied. 'After tonight, we will be safe, but tonight is terrible.'

Suddenly I thought of how frightened she would be if she saw the fight between the monster and myself. I asked her to go to bed. I would not go to her until I had discovered where my enemy was hiding.

She left me, and I walked through the house, searching

Chapter Twenty-one

everywhere. I did not find him. Suddenly I heard a dreadful
scream. It came from Elizabeth's room. As I heard it, I realized   15
the truth. She screamed again, and I ran into the room. Great
God! Why did I not die? Why am I here to tell you this terrible
tale? There she was, dead, lying across the bed, her head
hanging down, and her face covered by her hair. I fainted.

When I recovered, I was surrounded by the people of the   20
hotel. They had moved Elizabeth to another room. I escaped
from them to that room, ran to the bed where Elizabeth lay,
and embraced her. The marks of the devil's fingers were on
her neck.

Looking up, I saw the monster standing outside the open   25
window in the yellow moonlight. He grinned at me and
pointed at the body of my wife. I ran to the window, taking
the gun from my pocket, but he ran away at great speed and
jumped into the lake.

The sound of the gun brought people running into the   30
room. We searched for him for hours, but we did not find him.
I returned to the hotel, feeling sick with horror. Suddenly I
thought of my father. The monster might be going to him now.
He might murder my father. I decided to return to Geneva as
soon as possible.   35

On the journey back I wept. A devil had robbed me of every
hope of future happiness. No creature has ever been as
miserable as I was.

Frankenstein's Narrative Continues

When I arrived at Geneva, I found my father alive, but he
40 became ill when I told him the terrible news. He could not
live with the horrors that surrounded him. In a few days he
died in my arms.

What happened to me? I do not know. Sometimes I dreamt I
was walking in flowery fields with the people I loved, but I
45 awoke to find myself in prison. Slowly I recovered, and they
released me. They had called me mad, and I had spent many
months in a cell alone.

I thought I had no use for liberty, but slowly, as I
recovered, I began to want revenge. I was filled with a
50 maddening [1] anger when I thought of the monster. I began to
think of how I could get him. I went to a magistrate and told
him that I knew who had destroyed my family. I told my story
calmly, giving the dates and the places. I did not want him to
think I was mad. He listened to me, then he said, 'If the monster
55 is as you have described him, I will not be able to catch him.
He can live in caves of ice. He can run faster than any man. I
will try my best to arrest him, but I am afraid I will fail.'

'You do not care about my revenge,' I said. 'If you cannot
help me, I must pursue [2] him alone.'

60 He must have thought I was mad. He tried to calm me as a
nurse tries to calm a child. I left the house in anger.

1. **maddening** : that drives one mad.
2. **pursue** : follow.

1 Look back at Chapter 21 and complete the sentences below with the correct form of the verbs below:

> think (x2) feel become
> leave hear destroy go be (x2) catch
> spend believe die return

a. Victor .... that his father might be in danger.

b. While .... home, Victor .... miserable.

c. When Victor's father .... the terrible news he .... ill and eventually ....

d. Victor .... a long time in prison.

e. When Victor .... of the monster he .... filled with anger.

f. Victor .... to a magistrate and told him who .... his family.

g. The magistrate .... it .... impossible for him to .... the monster.

h. When Victor..........the magistrate's house he was angry.

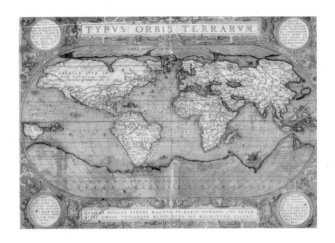

Chapter Twenty-two

R evenge alone gave me strength. I decided to
leave Geneva. I took my money and began the
travels that will end only with my death. I
have travelled all over the world. I have
5 suffered all the difficulties that travellers in
deserts and savage countries suffer. Often I have prayed for
death, but revenge has kept me alive. I could not die and leave
the monster living.

Before I left my home town forever, I visited the cemetery
10 where William, Elizabeth, and my father are buried. The night
was nearly dark. The spirits of my loved ones seemed to be
around me. They were dead, and I lived. Their murderer too
was alive, and I must keep living to destroy him. 'I swear,'

Chapter Twenty-two

said I, 'that I will find him and kill him, if he does not kill me first. Help me, good spirits, to find him. Help me to avenge you. Let him feel the despair that I feel now!'

In the silence of the night, I heard a loud and terrifying laugh. I felt as if hell were all around me. The laughter stopped and a voice said, 'I am content. You have decided to live, and I am content.'

I ran towards the sound, but I did not catch him. The moon came out from behind the clouds, and I saw him running away at amazing speed. I pursued him. For many months I have been following him. I pursued him over the Mediterranean and over the Black Sea. I followed him over Russia. Sometimes people who had seen him told me where he had gone. Sometimes he himself left some sign for me. He wants me to follow him. He is afraid I might despair and die. I travelled through snow. I saw the print of his great foot on

Frankenstein's Narrative Continues

the white ground. How can you, who are young and innocent,
40 understand what I felt? I was cold, tired, and hungry, but that
was nothing. I carried a hell inside me. Sometimes, when I
was dying of hunger, I found food. I think it was left there by
the good spirits who travelled with me. Often, when I was
thirsty, a few drops of rain would fall and relieve me.

45 I tried to follow the rivers, but the monster avoided them,
because there are more people by the river banks. In other
places I saw no human beings. I ate the wild animals that I
killed. I had money, and I gave it to the villagers to win their
help and friendship.

50 I was only happy when I slept. My good spirits gave me
sweet dreams. In sleep I saw William, Clerval, Elizabeth, and
my father again. Often, during the day, I told myself that I was
dreaming and would wake up that night with the people I
loved. At such moments, my revenge was more a duty than a
55 desire.

I do not know what the monster felt. Sometimes he left
messages written on the trees. 'Follow me to the frozen north,'
he wrote, 'where you will suffer but I will not. I have left a
dead rabbit for you. Eat. We will fight to the death, [1] but you
60 will suffer tortures before that moment arrives.'

---

1. **fight to the death** : fight until one of us is dead.

Chapter Twenty-two

I hate him! I will get my revenge! I will search for him until I die! Then how happy I will be to go to Elizabeth and the others. They are waiting for me!

As I travelled north, the weather became colder. The rivers were covered with ice, and I could get no fish. The monster was happy when I suffered. In one message he wrote, 'This is just the beginning! You will suffer much more than this!' 65

I bought a sledge and some dogs to pull it. In the sledge, I could move very quickly. I did not know if the monster had the same advantages, but every day I got closer to him. 70
I reached a village on the sea shore. There the people told me of a gigantic being who had taken food and a sledge with dogs.

Frankenstein's Narrative Continues

He had a gun, they said. He had set off in the sledge over the
sea of ice. They believed that the ice would break and he
75 would be killed.

I followed him. I do not know how many days have passed
since then. One day one of my dogs died of cold and fatigue.
I nearly despaired, but then I saw a dark speck in the distance.
It was him!

80 It was then that the ice broke. The sea rolled between me
and my enemy. I was left as you found me, on a floating sheet
of ice. If I die before he does, swear to me, Walton, that he will
not escape. Kill him for me! I do not ask you to follow him,
but, if he appears when I am dead, swear you will kill him! He
85 speaks well and his words might persuade you, as they once
persuaded me. Do not trust him. Remember the spirits of
William, Justine, Clerval, Elizabeth, my father, and your
unhappy Victor. Kill him. My spirit will be near to help you.

1 The following sentences (a-l) are unfinished. Match them with their right partners below, so as to complete them.

a. Victor could not die

b. After visiting the cemetery where his relations were buried

c. That night the monster said he was content

d. Victor had been following the monster

e. Sometimes the monster

f. While Victor was following the monster

g. Victor gave the villagers some money

h. As Victor was travelling north

i. By using a sledge Victor had bought

j. The monster was seen to

k. Suddenly the ice broke and Victor

l. Victor was left on the floating sheet of ice

1. the weather became colder.

2. because Victor had decided to live.

3. he felt hungry, thirsty and tired.

4. set off in a sledge over the sea of ice.

5. Victor swore he would kill the monster.

6. where Walton had found him.

7. was separated from his enemy by the sea.

8. he could move more quickly.

9. over the Mediterranean, the Black Sea and Russia for a long time.

10. because he did not want to let the monster live.

11. left a sign for Victor.

12. so as to receive some help.

𝔚𝔞𝔩𝔱𝔬𝔫'𝔰 𝔍𝔬𝔲𝔯𝔫𝔞𝔩 ℭ𝔬𝔫𝔱𝔦𝔫𝔲𝔢𝔰

26 August 17—

You have read this strange and terrifying story, Margaret. Do you feel your blood run cold as I do? Sometimes he could not continue his tale, he was so moved. At other times he

5 *spoke, but with difficulty. I could hear the pain in his voice.*

I wish I could comfort him, but I cannot. His only comfort now will be death. He believes that the spirits of his loved ones speak to him. What a wonderful man he must have been, before misery ruined him! One day he said to me, 'When I was

10 *young I thought I was destined for greatness, but now I know that, like Satan, I am chained to hell.'*

Walton's Journal Continues

*I wanted a friend, and I have found him, but I will lose
him now. I try to interest him in life, but he asks me, 'Can
any man be what Clerval was to me? Can any woman be
another Elizabeth? Even if I met people as good as they were,*   15
*it would not matter. We love the people we knew when we
were children. They know us as no later friend can know us.'*

2 September

My dear sister,
I am in danger, and I do not know if I will ever see   20
England again. I am surrounded by mountains of ice. There is
no escape. Perhaps the ice will destroy my ship. The crew look
to me for hope, but I have no hope to give them. If we all die,
my mad ambitions are the cause.
Frankenstein feels sorry for me. He tries to comfort me. His   25
words encourage the crew, but each day they become more
nervous, and I fear they will rebel.

Walton's Journal Continues

I do not think these papers will ever reach you. Even so,
30 *I must write about what has just happened. We are still*
surrounded by mountains of ice. It is very cold, and many of
my men have already died. Frankenstein grows weaker every
day. I wrote in my last letter that I was afraid that the crew
would rebel. This morning, as I sat with Frankenstein, some
35 *of the men came into the cabin. They told me that the crew*
wanted to return home. If the ice breaks, they want me to
promise that I will turn the ship southwards.

I had thought that Frankenstein was too ill to speak, but
he turned towards them and said, 'What are you saying? Did
40 *you not think that this was a glorious and honourable*
expedition? And why? Not because it was easy. It was
glorious and honourable because it was difficult, because it
was surrounded by danger, because it required all your
courage and strength. You dreamt of being remembered as
45 *brave men who had risked danger for the good of mankind.*
And now, when you face the first real danger, you want to go
home! You are ready to accept the shame of a defeat! Oh! Be
men! Be more than men! You can succeed if you have the
strength and the courage to do it. Go home as heroes, not as
50 *cowards who were afraid of the cold.'*

Walton's Journal Continues

The men were moved. They looked at one another. I said to them, 'Go back to your work and think about what has been said. If you still wish to go home, I will go. But I hope that your courage will return.'

They left the cabin. Frankenstein closed his eyes. 55

I do not know what will happen. I would rather die than return home in shame and defeat.

7 September

All is lost. I have agreed to go south if the ice breaks. I will come home a disappointed man. This is difficult to bear. 60

Walton's Journal Continues

12 September

   It is finished. I am returning to England. I have lost my
hopes of glory. I have lost my friend. On the ninth of
September the ice began to move. Frankenstein was very ill
65 *and could not leave his bed. On the eleventh the path to the*
south was free. I told Frankenstein that we were sailing for
England.
   'Are you really going home?' he asked.
   'Yes.'
70 *'Go home then, but I cannot.' He tried to get up but fell*
back on the bed. The doctor came to see him and told me that
he had only a few hours to live.
   I sat with Frankenstein. His eyes were closed, and I
thought he was asleep, but after a while he began speaking to
75 *me in a weak voice. 'I am dying, Walton, and the monster is*
still alive. I feel no hatred now. I no longer want revenge, but
my enemy must die. I have been thinking about all that I have
done. I do not think I was wrong. In a fit of madness I
created a rational creature. It was my duty to make him
80 *happy if I could, but I had another higher duty. I had a duty*
to my fellow human beings. I refused, and I was right to
refuse, to make a mate for the first creature. He was evil. He
killed my family. I should have destroyed him, but I failed.

Walton's Journal Continues

A few days ago I asked you to do it for me. Then I was full of anger and the desire for revenge. Now I ask you again, but this time I ask for good reasons.

'I feel death approaching. I see the spirits of my loved ones around me. I am going to them. Goodbye, Walton! Find your happiness in tranquillity. Do not be ambitious, even if your ambition is only the innocent one of making discoveries in science. But why do I say this? I have failed, but another may succeed.'

His eyes closed forever.

Margaret, what can I say about this death? How can I describe my sorrow? My eyes are full of tears... Wait a moment! What was that sound? It is midnight, but I can hear a voice coming from the room where Frankenstein's body lies. I must go and look. Goodnight, my sister.

Great God! An amazing thing has happened! I do not know if I can describe it, but I must. Without it this story would be incomplete.

I entered the room where Frankenstein's body lay. By the bed stood a creature I cannot find words to describe, a gigantic and horribly ugly figure. As he bent over the body, his face was covered by his long hair. His great white hand was stretched out towards Frankenstein, and he was speaking

85

90

95

100

105

words of grief and horror. When he heard me coming, he
moved towards the window. I asked him to stay.

110 He looked at me in surprise, then looked again at the body
of his creator. 'That is also my victim,' he said. 'His murder is
my last crime. My miserable life is finished. Oh, Frankenstein!
It is too late to ask your forgiveness.'

At first I thought that I should do as Frankenstein had
asked me and kill the monster. Now I felt pity for him, and I
115 was curious. I approached him. I did not dare to look at his
face. There was something frightening about his ugliness.
'Yes,' I said. 'It is too late. If you had wanted his forgiveness
before, Frankenstein would still be alive.'

'Do you think I did not feel sorry before? I hated my
120 crimes. They caused me great pain, but a dreadful selfishness
made me commit them. Once I was good, but misery made me
evil. That change caused me great pain. After the death of
Clerval, I returned to Switzerland. I pitied Frankenstein, and
I hated myself. But when I heard that he hoped to be happy, I
125 was filled with anger and envy. I was the slave of my own
revenge. After she died, evil became my good. The completion
of my evil plan was all I desired, and now it is complete.
There lies my last victim!'

I was moved by his words. Then I remembered

Walton's Journal Continues

Frankenstein's words: 'He speaks well and his words might   130
persuade you, as they once persuaded me. Do not trust him.'
When I looked at the dead body of my friend, I felt angry.
'Devil!' I said. 'How dare you come here and cry over your
crimes when it is too late! You feel no pity. You are only
miserable because you can torment him no longer.'   135

'No!' cried the monster. 'But I understand why you think
that. It does not matter what you think. I expect sympathy
from nobody. When I remember the crimes I have committed, I
cannot believe that I am the same creature who once was full
of love and goodness. The fallen angel becomes the devil.   140

'You have heard my story, but you have heard it from
Frankenstein, and he did not know everything. Even while I
destroyed his hopes, I was miserable. I still desired love and
friendship. I am a sinner, but all mankind sinned against me.

'It is true that I am evil. I murdered lovely and innocent   145
people. I ruined my creator. You hate me, but you do not hate
me as much as I hate myself.

'Now I will die. I will leave your ship on the ice raft that
brought me here. I will go to the most northern point of the
earth. I will burn myself to death, so that no one can learn   150
from my dead body how to create another like myself. I will
die. I will stop feeling misery. My creator is dead, and when I

too am dead we will both be forgotten. Years ago, when I
first felt the sunshine and heard the birds sing, I would have
155   been sorry to die. Now death is my only comfort.

     'Goodbye! I leave you, the last human being I will ever see.
Goodbye, Frankenstein! I caused you much pain, but I felt
more pain than you did.'

     He jumped from the cabin window onto the ice raft that
160   lay close to the ship. He soon disappeared from sight and was
lost in darkness and distance.

A C T I V I T I E S

1 Look back at Walton's journal entry for 26 August 17__ and find the synonyms for the words listed below.

unusual ....

scary ....

at times ....

go on ....

story ....

console ....

marvellous ....

destroyed ....

needed ....

2 In the letter dated 2 September say:

- how Walton feels
- how Frankenstein feels
- what Frankenstein tries to do
- how the crew feel

3 In the section dated 5 September Victor presented 3 reasons to the crew in order to persuade them to continue the expedition. List them here below. One has been written for you.

1. ....
2. It required courage and strength
3. ....

4 Look back at the section dated 12 September and complete the
following chart.

Time when the ice began to move	
Time when the way to the south was free	
How Victor was feeling	
What the Doctor said about Victor's condition	
What Victor had created	
What Victor had refused to create	
What Victor had asked Walton some days before	
What advice Victor gave to Walton	

5 Complete the following summary using the words below.

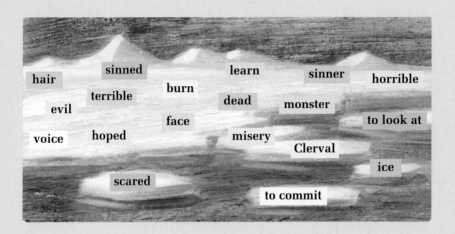

While writing in his journal, Walton's attention was drawn by a
.... coming from Frankenstein's room.

When Walton went there he saw a .... gigantic figure,
whose .... was covered by long ....

Walton did not dare .... the monster's face because he was
....

The monster admitted that a .... selfishness had led him
.... crimes and that .... had made him
....

Besides, he added that when he had been in Switzerland, after
.... 's death, he had felt envious because Frankenstein
.... to be happy.

He had become a .... because mankind had ....
against him.

Then the monster decided that he would .... himself so that
no one could .... how to create a new .... from his
.... body.

At the end the monster disappeared on an .... raft.

153

After reading the whole book

Characters

a. What do you think of the characters in the story?

b. Which of them do you sympathize with?

c. Do you believe that Victor is totally to blame?

d. Do you feel pity for the monster?

e. What would your behaviour be like in front of a monster or a deformed person? Would you be scared or would you be friendly?

f. Which of the characters do you think is most similar to Victor? Why? Give evidence to support your answers.

Pursuer and Pursued

All the story revolves around the theme of pursuit; there is, in fact, one character (the pursuer) who runs after another character (the pursued). Until Elizabeth's death Victor is pursued by the monster, then they exchange roles.
What causes this change? Why?

Narration - Narrators - Narratees

1 **The Narrator is the person who tells the story.**

☐ How many narrators have you met in the novel?

☐ Whose narration occupies the greater part of the novel?

☐ Whose narration is in epistolary form?

Complete:

The novel starts with some letters written by .... to his sister.

We understand that he is not the central character in the book: his presence is, in fact, functional.

Walton anticipates ....'s quest for new knowledge and ambition.

The greater part of the novel is told by ....: it is a sort of confession of his attempt to create the perfect being.

Within Victor's narrative there is the ....'s account of his life since when he was abandoned by ...., his creator.

So, there are .... different narrators in the novel.

2 **The sequence of narrators is symmetrical:**

Walton	(4 letters)
Victor	(Chapters 1-8)
Monster	(Chapters 9-14)
Victor	(Chapters 15-22)
Walton	(Journal)

The Narratee is the person to whom the story is told.
Complete the following charts.

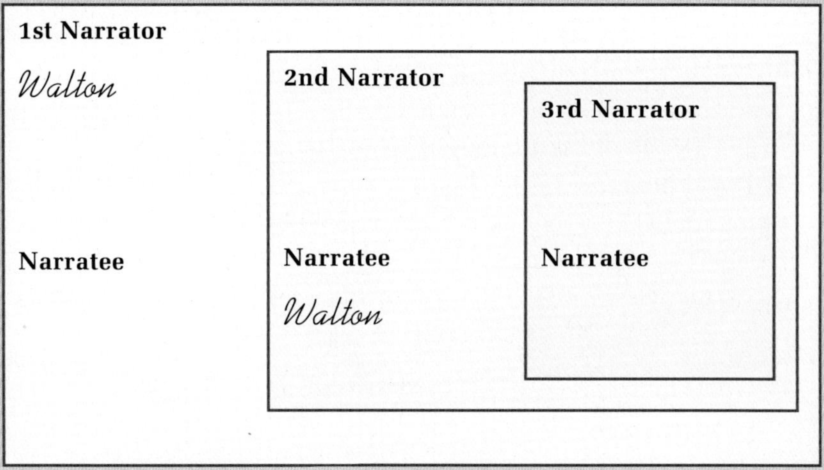

1st Narrator

Walton

2nd Narrator

3rd Narrator

Narratee

Narratee

Walton

Narratee

Story and Plot

Plot: is the way in which the author decides to present the events in a novel

Story: is the chronological sequence of the events

1 **The following is a list of the main events in the book, as presented by the author (Plot).**
Number them so as to put them in chronological order (Story).
Some of them have been done for you.

15 Walton sails to the North Pole

☐ Walton finds Victor Frankenstein

1 Frankenstein's childhood and adolescence

☐ Frankenstein creates a monster

☐ Frankenstein learns about William's death

☐ Justine is condemned

9 Frankenstein meets the monster on the Alps

☐ The monster comes to life

☐ The monster gets to De Lacey's cottage

☐ The monster learns to speak

6 The monster kills William

☐ Frankenstein decides to make a female creature

11 Frankenstein destroys the female creature

☐ Frankenstein is imprisoned after Clerval's death

☐ Frankenstein marries Elizabeth

☐ Elizabeth is killed by the monster

☐ Frankenstein dies

☐ Walton meets the monster who decides to abandon the world of men

2 Look at the following map and reconstruct Victor's movements throughout the story using arrows.

3 Look at the frontispiece of the edition of *Frankenstein* published in 1818 on page 7.

As you can see, the subtitle of the novel is *The Modern Prometheus*. It refers to the Greek myth of Prometheus which might be considered as a metaphor of the novel.

In the column on the left below you will find a brief description of the Prometheus myth.

Work with a partner and fill in the column on the right to compare Prometheus with Victor Frankenstein:

Prometheus	Victor Frankenstein
He was one of the Titans. He loved mankind.	He was a .... He loved ....
Zeus, the Father of Gods, refused to give mankind the gift of fire.	Only God and Nature had the .... to give life and ....
He stole a spark of fire from Zeus and gave it to mankind.	He stole the .... of life from Nature and made a .... to help mankind.
He was chained to a mountain.	He was punished for his .... against Nature and was compelled to .... a life of sufferings.
Every day a vulture ate Prometheus' liver which, however, grew again at night.	His punishment consisted of .... forever the creature he had made.

Can Victor Frankenstein's challenge be considered 'modern'? Why/why not?

Writing

Linking Literary Characters

Have you ever read *The Rime of the Ancient Mariner* by S. T. Coleridge?

In the long ballad, a mariner goes against the laws of Nature by killing an albatross and is consequently punished for his crime: he is condemned to a sort of life-in-death, because he has to wander all over the world and tell his story in expiation of his crime against Nature.

Could it be said that Victor and the mariner had something in common? Write a few lines on the topic.

The End of the Story

Did you like the end of the story? Why/why not?

Imagine a different ending and write it in your exercise book.

987 654 321